RECEIVED

OCT 2 8 2005

BY:_____

Y0-BCR-255
0 00 30 0386155 0

HAYNER PUBLIC LIBRARY DISTRICT
ALTON, ILLINOIS

MAIN

OVERDUES .10 PER DAY MAXIMUM FINE
COST OF BOOKS. LOST OR DAMAGED
BOOKS ADDITIONAL $5.00 SERVICE CHARGE.

DEAD FALL

DEAD FALL

Joan Lock

HAYNER PUBLIC LIBRARY DISTRICT
ALTON, ILLINOIS

This first world edition published in Great Britain 2005 by
SEVERN HOUSE PUBLISHERS LTD of
9–15 High Street, Sutton, Surrey SM1 1DF.
This first world edition published in the USA 2005 by
SEVERN HOUSE PUBLISHERS INC of
595 Madison Avenue, New York, N.Y. 10022.

Copyright © 2005 by Joan Lock.

All rights reserved.
The moral right of the author has been asserted.

British Library Cataloguing in Publication Data

Lock, Joan
    Dead fall
    1. Best, Ernest (Fictitious character) - Fiction
    2. Police - England - London - Fiction
    3. London (England) - Social conditions - 19th century - Fiction
    4. Detective and mystery stories
    I. Title
    823.9'14 [F]

    ISBN 0-7278-6244-8

Except where actual historical events and characters are being
described for the storyline of this novel, all situations in this
publication are fictitious and any resemblance to living persons
is purely coincidental.

Typeset by Palimpsest Book Production Ltd.,
Polmont, Stirlingshire, Scotland.
Printed and bound in Great Britain by
MPG Books Ltd., Bodmin, Cornwall.

mys
F
LOC

b16930903

To my good friend Mike Deeks
and the Branston Crime Circle

One

It is common knowledge that the Borough Market on a Saturday night is not a safe place for a lone policeman. Even one such as Detective Constable Jack Waters who is wearing inconspicuous private clothes. Indeed, it is particularly dangerous for him. If his identity is revealed he will be seen as a spy.

It is also common knowledge that costermongers hate policemen and can't wait for them to be drawn into a fight so they can all join in. Muzzling a copper is their favourite sport and one well worth serving time for.

Consequently, Waters tries not to attract attention as he pushes his way through the dregs of society who gather in the Borough Market at this hour: drunken roughs, prostitutes, pickpockets and the mostly unwashed poor.

He is almost deafened by the shouts of the stallholders trying to outdo each other promoting their dubious wares and the jingle-jangle of a piano organ relentlessly churning out popular tunes.

The occasional glimpse of a uniformed colleague in his snug, high-buttoned tunic brings some reassurance. Sensibly, these policemen inspect neither the merchandise nor the pedestrians too closely but maintain a remote and benign air. It does not take much to set off a riot in the Borough Market on a Saturday night.

Waters isn't exactly alone. But his companion, an informant named Clifford Armytage, is not only unlikely to be of any help in rescuing a policeman in trouble but his appearance does attract attention.

Armytage is very much the toff with his cream cashmere overcoat and his black, shallow-crowned bowler with its sharply curved brim. The fact that he has just revealed that he is carrying a revolver unsettles Waters even more.

The pair come to a halt outside a paint-shy green door next to a greengrocer's shop that is still doing brisk business. The detective makes it plain that he thinks they are wasting their time looking for the wanted man in there.

Armytage sighs and insists that, this time, they will catch him.

'Leave it to *me*,' he mutters contemptuously.

As he is speaking, the green door opens and a middle-aged couple and a young man emerge.

The older man has a jaunty but slightly nervous air while the younger one is cheerful but appears somewhat frail. The woman, who carries a shopping basket, is plump and of a homely but spirited aspect. All three are dressed rather more colourfully and cheerfully than the rest of the crowd. They are the strolling players, Mr and Mrs Jarvis and their son, Shakespeare.

After they have moved away, Clifford Armytage approaches the green door and raps on it sharply. Looking back, Mrs Jarvis notices the elegant stranger at her door. While her nervous husband bolts into a pub, she pulls her shawl around her in the manner of many a beleaguered stage heroine, and goes over to enquire what he wants.

Assuming a compassionate manner, Armytage explains to her that he is a friend of the poor couple who had been staying with them and he wants to help them.

Mrs Jarvis gives him a look of disgust.

'We've discovered that the husband is a bad lot,' she says indignantly, 'an escaped convict in fact! That has already brought trouble with the police on to Mr Jarvis.'

She straightens her shoulders, pulls her shawl more tightly around her, and declares, 'We want nothing more to do with either of them lest we be charged with harbouring!'

Then off she goes, like the other women shoppers, to buy the makings of their Sunday dinner.

Suddenly, a panicky Mr Jarvis arrives, mopping his brow, then dropping his handkerchief in his confusion. He takes out his key and proceeds to open the green door.

Armytage and Waters manage to confuse him over his hand-kerchief. The flustered man is vaguely aware of danger, so assumes an air of nonchalance, pretends he does not live above the greengrocer's and wanders off again, quite forgetting about the key.

A triumphant Armytage uses the key to gain entrance then re-emerges, hands it to Waters and tells him to fetch more police.

'If they're here, I'll give the signal, then come in at once.'

Inside the flat at the top of the stairs, are the escaped convict, Harold, and his wife, Bess. He is dark and handsome in a very strong and manly way, with a broad chest and powerful shoulders. She, though frail and poorly dressed, is blonde and beautiful.

They are eagerly awaiting the arrival of Seth Preene, who, by telling the truth about his part in Harold's downfall, will exonerate him. They hear sounds on the stairs.

'It's Preene!' Bess exclaims excitedly. She rushes towards the door, opens it then slams it shut again.

'No! It's Clifford Armytage!' she shouts in horror and flings the bolt across.

Eventually she lets Armytage in, pretending that Harold has escaped. But the man's insults soon draw the fugitive out of hiding. Clifford is Harold's cousin, and the man who not only committed the crime of which he was accused but also stole Harold's inheritance.

Harold's pent-up anger is matched by Clifford's frustration at Harold's determination to escape the net he has so care-fully spun around him. Fierce and furious fisticuffs ensue.

The fighting pair burst through into the back-parlour. Clifford, realizing he is getting the worst of it, draws his revolver, but Harold snatches it from him, makes him kneel and holds the weapon to his head.

Suddenly, there is a loud banging on the flat door and the voice of Detective Waters is heard shouting, 'Police! Open the door!'

Harold now feels he has nothing to lose. He will never get justice.

'If you speak one word you are a *dead man*!' he hisses at Clifford.

The next moment, the parlour is filled with policemen. Clifford makes a plunge for the revolver which goes off.

This acts as a rallying cry to the crowd gathering outside. They begin to murmur their disapproval of police action.

Harold dashes to the back-parlour window, opens it and leaps out on to the roof of the cobbler's stall just below. From there, he jumps on to the ground and begins to run.

His way is blocked by a police inspector and a constable. He fights them desperately, knocking them both to the ground but he is grabbed from behind and held by Waters. Harold, the escaped convict, so close to finding justice, is recaptured.

The crowd begin to bunch and yell: 'Let 'im go!'

'He ain't done nothing!'

'Bleedin' rozzers!'

'Let's 'ave 'em!'

They advance menacingly, their cries ugly and deafening. They are halted for a moment by a pistol shot. More rabble pour in from all directions sensing the opportunity for a fight. More police follow.

All hell breaks loose.

Knives and coshes emerge, fists fly, raucous shouts blend with bloodcurdling screams and the crunch of boots finding their targets.

There is a riot.

The music swells to a dramatic crescendo while the lights are lowered, blacking out the scene.

Helen leans over to Best, who is sitting beside her in the Princess's Theatre stalls.

'Realistic, is it?'

'Absolutely,' he laughs. 'It was like that every Saturday night in the Borough Market. Worse, sometimes!'

Two

Gradually the lights come up again to reveal the interior of a police station. There are 'Wanted for Murder' posters on the walls and, to the right, a prisoners' dock. A uniformed constable wheels on a desk behind which an inspector immediately takes up position.

More policemen are spread around the room. Eight of them are wearing uniform and two, Detectives Waters and Cutts, are in private clothes. Alongside Waters stands the elegant Clifford Armytage looking triumphant as Harold and Bess are dragged in. Harold is placed in the dock, facing the inspector.

Hovering on the edge, to the left of the police station set, are the rabble. They are being restrained by more policemen. Even while the lights were lowered they had kept up their baying but it now becomes a little fainter so that the actors might be heard above them.

In order that the audience remains aware of their continuing menace, however, the inspector turns towards the restraining policemen and shouts urgently, 'Keep the crowd back! Keep them back!'

'Courage, Bess,' Harold calls out from the dock. 'Seth Preene hasn't forgotten us.' He points accusingly to his cousin. 'It is Clifford Armytage who is at the bottom of this.'

Armytage eyes him disdainfully.

Bess runs over to Armytage, kneels before him and starts to beg, 'Please spare my husband . . .'

A long piercing scream from among the crowd drowns out the rest of her line. Another follows.

Then there are shouts of horror:

'Oh my God!'

5

'No!'

'What's happened?!'

'Look here! Look here!'

Bess stops, confused. She glances around her for guidance. Her expression is asking whether this is some new 'business' that she's not been told about.

The rest of the cast freeze, caught in mid-action as if in one of those Frith paintings of life on Derby Day or at the railway station. Those actors facing to the left stare towards the crowd, which appears to be turning in on itself.

Then it begins moving away from its centre to stare at the space at the edge of the stage. There, spreadeagled, face downwards, lies a costermonger. Best cannot see which one.

The rabble now begins to disintegrate in confusion. Actors gesticulate towards the wings, two of them leaning over the costermonger, trying to rouse him.

A frock-coated gentleman rushes on, takes one glance at the figure lying immobile on the stage, then signals feverishly to the hovering workmen in the wings. They promptly bring down the curtain with an unseemly crash.

A stunned silence falls over the audience. They begin looking at each other, at first perplexed, then audibly voicing the question, what on earth is going on?

Since no answers are forthcoming from the stage feverish speculation takes hold of the two thousand people packed into the vast auditorium. Their voices swell.

Some of those perched up in the dizzyingly high gods begin shouting down to the middle-class families in the steeply raked circles. The pittites, who always think they own the place anyway, begin to stand up and move about. Some go forwards from their seats at the rear of the auditorium towards the front stalls and the stage.

'Hey, what's going on?' one of them shouts.

'Has someone died, or something?' yells another.

Helen and Best are as puzzled as everyone else. They know this is definitely not in the script. Certainly wasn't when Helen witnessed a rehearsal which introduced changes to that scene. Was this then a Wilson Barrett stunt meant to heighten the realism for which the play was already famed?

A ripple at the centre of the curtains causes the audience to grow quieter and the emergence of Waters, the Detective, brings an expectant hush. But he says nothing, merely stands peering around.

Voices begin to be raised again only to be hushed. 'Let's hear what 'e's goin' to say.'

But he still doesn't say anything. Then his eyes light upon what he is seeking and he leaves the stage, descends into the auditorium and hastens towards the end of Best's row. There he stops, hands a note to the man in the last seat and points towards Best.

As he reads the scribbled note and begins to rise, Best whispers to Helen, 'They need my help backstage. I'll be back as soon—'

'No, I'm coming with you,' she says firmly, getting up and moving along the row with him before he can argue. 'I suspect you are going to need all the help you can get.'

The first thing to strike Best as he stepped on to the stage was the acrid smell and the overpowering heat from the lights.

The heat from stage lighting was never pleasant for the audience and one of the drawbacks of the spectacular theatre was the love affair with lighting – both gas and lime. Some playgoers even refused to attend the evening performance following a matinee due to the build-up of heat and smell in the auditorium.

The atmosphere onstage now, with the curtains down, resembled a rather noxious Turkish bath. Small wonder the actors all had a sheen of perspiration over their garish make-up.

The second thing Best noticed was that the body was that of the chestnut seller. His cap was no longer on his head but lying nearby on the ground and his red neckerchief was now wet, the wet redness spreading outwards in a large pool around his head.

'He's dead,' announced a portly, middle-aged gentleman withdrawing his stethoscope from the man's chest.

Best was not surprised. With a hole like that in the back of the victim's head, he could have made that diagnosis. The hole was neat and round but when they turned the man over the exit wound was neither. It was wide and ragged and ugly in the extreme.

Best's mind was racing. What to do first? This was nothing like the average incident where you arrived at a scene and began by asking what has happened here, sir, please?

Everyone could see what had happened but, despite all the potential observers, could anyone tell him how? Or why? Or who had done it?

He made some instant decisions.

'Three things,' he said to Kite, the Assistant Stage Manager who was so agitated that such a thing should happen on the night he was left in charge that he kept swaying from one foot to the other so that Best thought he might faint.

'Yes. Yes.'

'First, send a messenger to Marlborough Street Police Station and tell them that we need all the help we can get.' Thank goodness it was only five minutes away. He paused. 'Have you got a telegraph machine?'

Kite nodded. 'But it's in the office and that's locked.'

'Break down the door,' ordered Best peremptorily, 'find a telegrapher and send a message to Scotland Yard Detective Branch telling them what has happened and requesting immediate assistance.'

Probably a waste of time, he thought. They would have all gone home by now and he'd have to make do with divisional detectives. The ASM hesitated. He was unaccustomed to acting entirely on his own authority and without a basic script. He kept looking around for someone.

'Do it!' exclaimed Best.

'All right. All right.' The ASM beckoned an actor.

'No. No actors,' said Best, waving the actor back. 'Send stagehands.' He paused, took a deep breath and continued. 'Third, I want all the actors to assume the positions they were in when the shot was heard.'

At this there was some discontented murmuring.

'Oh, I don't know *exactly* where I was, do I?'

'One is moving so fast in this scene.'

'Approximately, then,' snapped Best.

They began shuffling about.

'I was there, just behind Waters,' said the hokey-pokey man.

'No, you weren't, *I* was,' insisted a particularly unlovely, wall-eyed tramp. 'You were upstage. Like you always are,' he added with a hint of malice.

The voice of Wilson Barrett cut in quietly to enquire, 'What shall we do about the audience?'

Barrett, who up to now had only been quietly watching the proceedings, not only took the part of the hero, Harold Armytage, in *The Lights o' London* but, like so many male leads these days, was also the powerful actor-manager. Why hadn't he stepped in earlier? Was that whom Kite had been looking around for?

'Should we send them home?'

Best and Helen glanced at each other in horror.

'Oh, God,' said Best.

'Two thousand potential witnesses,' nodded Helen.

'Keep them here until the police arrive from Marlborough Street. Then have an officer at each exit taking names and asking them what they saw.'

'That will take all night,' said Helen, 'and they will tell lies so they can go home.'

'What do *you* suggest, then?' he asked a little testily. She was the light of his life but did have an unnerving habit of voicing uncomfortable truths.

'They should do as you say,' she agreed, 'but also,' she turned to Kite, 'issue them all with free tickets for a special matinee performance. They won't be able to resist. Seeing it again might jog their memories so we can get more out of them.'

'Free tickets!' exclaimed the ASM.

'Yes,' said Best. 'Well, they're not seeing the full play tonight, are they? And let's face it, the publicity will make this theatre a fortune.'

Barrett pursed his lips thoughtfully then nodded, 'A good idea.'

'Even the Dead Heads who never paid to get in in the first place?'

9

Helen and Best raised their eyebrows at each other.

Wilson Barrett looked pained but said, '*Especially* the Dead Heads. They will be so thrilled at not having to queue for hours in the hope of getting in for free that they are bound to respond.'

Best pondered then said, 'We'd better tell the policemen to be particularly thorough with the toffs in the stalls – and to process them first.'

'Yes,' agreed Barrett. '*They* won't be so easily bought.'

Best turned his attention back to the victim. 'Now,' he said, 'who is this man?'

'I don't know,' said Kite.

Best looked at Barrett, who shrugged his powerful shoulders and said, 'Nor do I, Inspector.'

Three

'You don't know who he is?!' exclaimed Best. 'How can you not know who he is when he is performing in your theatre every night?'

'He's a supernumerary,' murmured Barrett quietly, 'a walk-on.' He inclined his head and added, 'They come and go. The Super Master recruits them. He has all their personal details.'

Best turned to the ASM and directed, 'Find the Super Master.'

Kite glanced at Barrett, who nodded his assent, then pointed to a stagehand, who hurried off importantly.

'Meanwhile,' said Best, who was still desperately trying to decide what to do next without revealing his confusion, 'tell me which one of you held the gun last?'

He pointed to the weapon that lay on the stage at the centre of a wide circular space that had mysteriously opened up around it. This, despite the fact that the cast were all now supposedly in the same positions as when it was last fired. They were disowning it and with it any contamination or suggestion of guilt.

'I did, of course,' said Barrett, 'but I dropped it as I made my leap through the window.'

'Was that intended – that you do that – let go of the gun?'

'Yes. After I landed on the stage but it didn't always work out that way. Sometimes it fell out of my hand as I jumped on to the roof of the cobbler's shop. It would end up inside the back parlour or tumble down the roof on to the ground outside.'

They all gazed at the offending weapon now clearly yards away from the window.

'And this time?'

He lifted his muscular shoulders.

'Not sure. Outside I think.'

Best frowned.

All very convenient. This experienced performer not knowing when the gun would fall from his grasp?

'It's not a real gun though, is it? Just an imitation?'

'Absolutely. Should be. Certainly didn't feel any different tonight.'

'Does it *look* any different?'

They both stared at the firearm that lay on the floor between them. The blue metal revolver certainly looked real enough with its long, narrow barrel and elegantly swept-back handle mounted with an etched walnut grip.

Best picked it up and weighed it in his hand. It felt real too. Heavy and solid.

He took it over to Barrett, who looked it over carefully, then he also weighed it in his right hand.

He shook his head.

'No, this is not the same one we use in the play,' he said.

The firearm *was* disturbingly familiar to Best, however. It was very similar to the .450 Adams breech-loaders hurriedly issued to the Metropolitan Police after the Clerkenwell Prison Explosion.

Fenians had tried to free one of their own condemned prisoners and, as a result, over six hundred Adams breech-loading

.450 revolvers had been supplied from Army stores in the Tower of London.

Not that the officers on the beat had seen much of them. Superintendents, frightened of the responsibility of having them around, promptly locked them away. Senior officers then announced to the Press that the police did not want to be armed.

In fact, most constables on night beats in dangerous areas would have been grateful for the comfort of a revolver, particularly now that so many burglars had taken to carrying firearms. If poor old PC Atkins had had a pistol he might not have been killed while disturbing one of them only a week ago, reflected Best. He did not dare to contemplate what it meant if this *was* one of the police issue.

Wilson Barrett moved over to look at the anonymous victim. The other actors took it that they could move from their allotted places.

'No!' exclaimed Best waving them back. 'Stay where you *are* . . .'

This was hopeless. He needed to have them searched before they left the stage. The original gun must be *somewhere*. Also, to question them. But first he also had to note where they all stood at this moment. He sighed and turned to Barrett.

'Have you some chalk, so we can mark their places?' He knew that was sometimes done at rehearsals so that actors would resume their correct positions.

The stocky, all-powerful actor-manager thought for a minute then suggested, 'Might be a better idea if we got out the camera we use to photograph the performances? Then we can – ' he smiled – 'freeze them in their places for all eternity?'

'Splendid idea,' agreed Best with a laugh. He looked around the cast. 'Got that? Stay exactly where you are just for a few minutes more.'

Nods and resigned shrugs greeted this latest instruction.

'When that's done I'd like you all to gather at – er . . .'

'In the Green Room?' suggested Barrett.

'Yes, good idea. But before you leave the stage you will all have to be searched – when sufficient men have arrived.

My wife, here, and the lady dressers will search the actresses.'

This brought some sighing, groaning and shifting about from foot to foot, which was soon quelled by a sharp glance from Barrett. Obviously the man ran a tight ship.

'But they can go to their dressing rooms to remove their make-up before they go to the Green Room?' he enquired.

Best pondered for a moment.

'I don't see why not. Once they've been searched. I want to talk to you first anyway.'

'Very well. As soon as we have taken the photograph and I've been searched, we'll go to my dressing room, where we can talk while I remove my make-up.' He glanced over at Kite. 'Send the Super Master along – *when* you find him.'

Best sensed a hint of exasperation. He guessed that the Super Master, like many theatre folk, was over-fond of alcohol.

Best wanted to ensure that the actors did not discuss the incident between themselves but saw little hope of that. Instead he merely warned, 'Remember we want to know what *you* saw and heard not what one of your colleagues tells you happened.'

'Absolutely,' agreed Barrett. 'It is important to us to establish the truth.' He looked around them with a warning eye. No keeping back information to protect a friend.'

He paused for gravitas then added, 'Until we find the killer we are all suspects and our livelihoods are at stake. Perhaps, while you are waiting,' he added, 'you might each like to make some notes as to what you saw. Right, Mr Best?'

Best nodded.

These detective tales in *The Strand* magazine had a lot to answer for. The man was being most helpful and co-operative but Best could see that, if he wasn't careful, Barrett might take over the proceedings. After all, the man was accustomed to being in charge.

Well, so am *I*, thought Best, and this is *my* performance even though the role is a particularly strange one.

Four

During the course of his work Best had had cause to enter several theatrical dressing rooms. Even in the better theatres he'd found them to be cramped, dimly lit, poorly furnished and quite depressing.

Those in the splendid new Princess's Theatre, however, were a revelation. Little wonder that the theatrical Press celebrated these as 'civilized' for a change.

Not only were there a great many of them – no fewer than thirty-two, spread over three floors – but all that he glanced into as he passed appeared spacious, well lit and handsomely furnished.

None more so, of course, than that of the actor-manager, which almost opened on to the stage, it was so close. Nearby, were two more dressing rooms, the only others on the ground floor. One was for the leading lady, Miss Eastlake. The other was used by both Wilson Barrett's brother, George, who played the jaunty but nervous Mr Jarvis, and E. S. Willard, – the villain of the piece, Clifford Armytage.

All the lead actors who needed hasty and frequent changes of costume. Best noted this. It could be important. One of them may also have wanted to change guns rapidly.

Although something of a dandy himself, Best still found it incongruous to see such an obviously manly man spreading handfuls of cream across his handsome face as he removed his make-up.

Wilson Barrett was the son of an Essex farmer and, at the age of thirty-five and after many years in the theatre, still retained something of the air of a son of the soil. But a singularly attractive and forceful country lad, however.

What was it, the Detective Inspector wondered, that so drew

14

your eyes to this actor and kept them there – off-stage as well as on?

Was it merely his good looks and well-muscled body? His air of pent-up energy? Perhaps it was that he moved so well for such a sturdy man or that his voice, while deep and actorly, was admirably clear and resonant, allowing him to sound strong in high drama but soft and gentle when tenderness was called for.

Most likely it was the sum of all these parts – plus being responsible for an enormous success. An attractive man at the top of his profession.

Small wonder the ladies all adored him.

But why did he not appear more worried by the tragedy? He had so much to lose. Did he believe in himself so much that he felt invincible? Had he so many friends in high places who would shield him?

Or was it because the murder onstage could only add to the popularity of this latest dramatic sensation?

After all, so much had been made of the play's remarkable realism this would certainly add to it. Many newspapers hailed *The Lights o' London* as a wonderful breakthrough in realistic theatre, particularly in the handling of the crowd scenes.

This was a skill hitherto thought to be the sole prerogative of the German company, the Meiningers. The Press were pleased to see the British competing by way of (as *The Illustrated London News* put it) 'realism out-realized'.

Oddly, at the same time many reviewers not only found little new in the plot but wondered why on earth the public might wish to be entertained with an accurate depiction of the squalor and degradation they could see for themselves in the real Borough Market or 'The Cut' every Saturday night.

Why, they exclaimed in horrified chorus, you could almost feel the greasy grit and grime and smell the putrid smells. And this was supposed to be entertainment!

Whatever the reason for its great popularity, Best knew that *The Lights o' London* was exactly the resounding success that the huge new Princess's Theatre on Oxford Street had so desperately needed.

It was common knowledge that it had not had a full house since the opening in November 1880. Even the famous American actor, Edwin Booth, the melancholic brother of the man who had assassinated President Lincoln, had failed to draw crowds to see his Hamlet.

Matters only began to improve when Mr Wilson Barrett arrived from the Royal Court and he set about reviving some of his past successes.

But only with the current play, written by reforming journalist G. R. Sims, did the new theatre have a hit which filled its many seats and made people desperate for tickets. Might others be desperate to ruin it?

'Have you any enemies?' Best shot at Barrett suddenly.

The actor-manager's hand halted on its way across the sharp planes of his cheek. His eyes met Best's with a smile.

'Of course!' he exclaimed. 'This is the theatre. We're all the best of friends and the worst of enemies. Green room gossip is lethal, I can tell you!'

Barrett grimaced at his reflection in the dressing-table mirror, holding his head back to stretch his neck as he removed the last traces of ruddy glow while with the other hand he whipped away his protective towel.

Best smiled. Such fluid theatrical moves, all beautifully executed. You could swear they had been rehearsed many times over.

He was surprised to see how pale Barrett's skin now looked.

'We don't get out much,' the actor grinned, reading Best's mind, 'and the atmosphere in the theatre is – well – rotten.'

'No particular enmity raging at the moment though?' asked Best, coming back to his question.

Barrett shook his head. 'As you know, the Lyceum is our only professional rival – but it's a friendly rivalry. Indeed, we need each other. A hit at one theatre can help the other. People become enthused about the theatre, so go more often.'

Sounded reasonable. Too reasonable?

There was a sharp rat-tat on the door. It opened to reveal the doctor, who announced unceremoniously, 'That man's body is covered with bruises.'

16

Five

The dreary clothes of Bess, the care-worn wife, could not disguise the seductive blonde beauty of the actress, Miss Mary Eastlake, who played her.

She stood before Helen pale and trembling and said, 'It's terrible, just terrible. That poor man!'

Helen observed that Mary was the only one of these self-obsessed people who seemed to be really upset about the death. The rest, after the initial shock, seemed to be irritated by the inconvenience or worried about the possible effects it might have on the popularity of their production.

'Did you know him?' Helen asked as she took the girl's shawl and helped her remove her blouse. Mary's corset looked too amply filled by her creamy bosom to allow room for any hidden object, particularly one as large as a pistol. Nonetheless, Helen made sure that that was the case.

'No! No, I didn't know him. Or, at least, I don't think I did! There are so many people in this play,' she added nervously as she pulled up her skirt so that Helen could check underneath.

Her hands were shaking. Helen doubted that this was due to embarrassment. Actresses were accustomed to undressing in front of others. But it was evident that the air of vulnerability essential for the role of Bess was also part of Mary's own character – or perhaps her confidence had been shaken by the reviews?

Amidst all the praise heaped on the cast of *The Lights o' London* only Mary Eastlake, Barrett's new leading lady, had been found wanting.

The Theatre had declared her perfect as 'the poor, hunted, wayworn, loving Bess', but opined that she 'failed in force

17

when called upon in scenes of passionate intensity'.

Other commentators followed suit:

'Not strong enough for such exhibitions of abandoned emotion.'

'Overstrung . . . and at times lacking in physical power.'

'Shrill.'

And (not surprisingly given her reception in the part) 'nervous' and 'anxious' at times.

Only the *Punch* critic was sympathetic to the young actress's dilemma. They pointed out that throughout the play she'd been called upon to be fatigued, fainting, half-dying and 'being perpetually carried about or being embraced by Mr Wilson Barrett, who is invariably soothing her, or consoling her, or sending her off to sleep, or keeping her quiet in a general way – which is not conducive to much development of speech'.

Despite this, they had added, Mary Eastlake had made 'the most of her single opportunity of giving the villain a piece of her mind at the end of the piece'.

As well she might, Helen had muttered when she read the review. She was also of the opinion that some of this venom could justly have been directed at Mr G. R. Sims, the playwright with a conscience. As *Punch* had pointed out, the only other girl character, the wanton Hetty Preene, 'was soon out of it altogether'.

In fact there was another young actress with a substantial and spirited role, Miss Esther Gibbons. She had received reviews describing her acting as cheery, natural and clever. But she was playing a boy, Shakespeare Jarvis.

Helen held the blouse so that Mary could slide her arms back in, then gave her a handkerchief to help soak up her tears. Were these not, she wondered, a little excessive for someone the girl purported not to know?

She was tempted to make a kind remark about Mary's performance but decided that this might appear false and patronizing in the circumstances. Instead she patted the girl's arm and said, 'You've been very helpful. Thank you. Perhaps you could help me with the children now?'

Mary nodded gratefully.

* * *

Harold Smart, the Princess's Theatre Super Master, did indeed have details of all the supernumeraries or walking ladies and gentlemen. The victim, he revealed by perusing his alphabetically arranged register, was Albert George Talisman.

'That's a striking name,' said Best.

Smart sniffed. 'Made up, probably. They think callin' themselves something peculiar like that makes 'em more memorable.'

Best thought they could be right although in this instance it clearly hadn't worked.

'What else can you tell me about him?'

Smart ran his bony forefinger across the page. 'Aged thirty-two. Height five-foot-eight. Hair dark an' curly. No side-whiskers or beard. Curly moustache. Good teeth. Can walk.'

Best furrowed his brow.

'Need to 'ave good teeth in case 'e has to be a supernumerary gentleman,' Smart explained. 'Bad teeth and gaps is all right for poor folk or a crowd of roughs like you saw we 'ad on stage 'ere tonight.'

He looked Best over. 'You'd be a good walking gentleman,' he said, taking in the sparkling white molars and his fashionable high-fastening, single-breasted jacket with its narrow shawl collar and revers. ''Specially of the foreign variety.'

Best smiled. The man was exactly right about the latter. He was half Italian and judged by some of his colleagues as being just a little bit flashy and exotic looking.

'Can walk? What does that mean? Not crippled?'

'Oh no. No!' Smart laughed knowingly. Pulling his gaunt frame up to its full height of around six foot, he proceeded to explain the mysteries of his trade to an ignorant and uninitiated detective.

'Means they can walk the stage – an' look right when they're doin' it. Holding their arms properly – not stiff down by their sides like nor swinging about too much either. It's the arms an' hands what trip up a lot of the blokes. They doesn't know what to do with them, do you see. An' they should walk on the balls of their feet – so they can turn quickly without falling over.' He demonstrated a shaky turn probably aided more by the alcohol in his bloodstream than how his weight was distributed.

'Now your walking "ladies".' Smart was in full flood now. 'They've got to be able to look right in elegant dresses and handle the skirts and trains proper – as if they was born to wear 'em.'

Best thought: In my innocence, I was under the impression that once you'd acquired the skill of walking as a child nothing could be more natural – on stage or off. But apparently this was not the case. That is one of the beauties of this job, he thought. You discover curious facts and learn a lot about the strangeness of human beings.

'Anything else?'

Smart glanced at a column on the right-hand side of his register.

'Yeah. He would have been all right for thinking parts and as an understudy to a utility.' He paused. 'A "gentleman" utility, that is.'

Best rolled his eyes and gave Smart a look of supplication which actually made the dour man laugh.

'Thinking parts is when you're just there on the stage doing nothing – just sitting there or standing there – thinking. Not lookin' like an idiot but like you had something going on in your 'ead. Like you're a wise man an' that sort of thing.'

Best nodded but remained a trifle perplexed. Surely anyone could do that?

Smart read his mind. 'Might not seem like much but you 'as to have a bit up 'ere for that,' he said, pointing his right forefinger at his forehead.

'Be a bit smart, in fact?' grinned Best.

'That's right! That's right!' Smart laughed immoderately, sending a blast of whisky fumes towards Best as he did so. 'Or look as if you 'ave.'

Which is not always the same thing, as Best knew from his contact with senior officers.

'And these "gentleman" utilities?'

'Well, utilities is little speaking parts an' sometimes, if they're lucky, a super might get to understudy one.'

'And Talisman was lucky?'

'No,' Smart said quickly. 'But he could have been – if one was needed. If a utility bloke was sick or something an' they

20

came and asked me who could do it – fill in like at short notice. He'd be one of them I'd say.'

'But only for "gentlemen"?'

'Far as I know. Might 'ave been able to do a Cockney or something else.'

'So, Talisman spoke like a "gentleman"?'

This was as drawn out as the business of waiting for your expenses to be approved by the Receiver.

'Yes. Bit like a toff he was.' Smart sniffed. 'We're gettin' quite a few of them, you know – stage-struck toffs wanting to be supernumeraries but at least they're not trying to push their way in as actors like some does.'

Best knew that this was a cause of much resentment among actors who had worked their way up the hard way: toffs getting acting jobs through their connections. A price of the increasing respectability of the profession, he supposed.

So, thought Best, 'a wider picture' was emerging, as Chief Inspector Cheadle would say. We now have a middle-class or upper-class supernumerary who looked bright but might not be, had good teeth, a curly moustache and could walk.

'Where did he live?'

'Bloomsbury.'

Ah, that was a relief. Bloomsbury was only ten minutes walk away.

'I've heard that these supernumeraries come and go.'

'Well, you've 'eard wrong,' said Smart crisply. He seemed so offended by the suggestion, the red spots high on his cheekbones were getting redder. 'Not in a proper 'ouse like this nor in a show like this. They got to be trained, you know. Every move is worked out an' practised and practised. That's why everyone says our crowd scenes is the best ever,' he added proudly as if he himself had choreographed and rehearsed all the moves.

'So you have all the same people you had on the opening night?'

'Well, I wouldn't say that.' Smart shrugged his spare shoulders.

Well, for God's sake what *would* you say?! thought Best, who was struggling to maintain the necessary patient and attentive expression.

'Of course, some drops out – sick an' that. We even,' Smart confided almost proudly, 'had one who died of an 'eart attack . . .'

'And Talisman?' prompted Best. 'Was he here at the start?' He looked down at his register.

'No.'

Best clenched his hands, making his nails dig deep into his palms.

''E had worked for us before. Last time was – let's see . . .' Smart consulted his book in a leisurely fashion, 'in *Branded* before Mr Barrett came here. But that show didn't last long . . .'

The attentive smile was making Best's jaw seize up.

'And *this* time?'

'This time . . .' More consultation of his supers bible. 'This time – he started 'ere about a week ago.' He stopped suddenly, looked again and said, 'No. I tell a lie,' his finger stabbing at the book, ' – four days ago. Took the place of a bloke that broke 'is leg.'

'On stage? He broke his leg while on stage?'

Smart nodded. 'These things 'appen, you know.'

It seems they did – at this theatre – in this play, thought Best.

'Of course,' he nodded understandingly. 'Is that why,' he began but stopped suddenly. He'd been about to ask: Is that why Talisman had bruises all over his body? These 'things' which kept happening? But he changed his mind.

He'd keep that fact to himself for the present.

Six

Best was back where he had been earlier in the evening except this time it was the cast of *The Lights o' London*

22

who sat in the front stalls while Best stood looking down at them from the 30-foot-wide stage of the Princess's Theatre.

For two reasons he had decided against addressing the gathering in the Green Room. Firstly, because he felt that the actors were just too scattered, casual and comfortable in there. Indeed, some of them had already been asleep when he arrived.

This was a serious business and he wanted their full attention to drive it home. Placing them where their audience usually sat might wake them up a little. Disturb them, even.

As it happened, now that he stood up there looking out over this vast and sumptuous auditorium, he got the feeling that it was only he who was disorientated. How on earth did the actors manage to act naturally in a setting that made one feel so Lilliputian?

The other reason he had deserted the Green Room, although he would have been loathe to admit it, was to demonstrate to Mr Wilson Barrett just who was in charge here. Charming though the man was, Best felt that this point needed to be made. Now he just felt foolish.

'I appreciate that you are tired,' he announced – but he couldn't hear his own voice! What was happening? If he couldn't hear it how could the actors out there? He took a deep breath and almost shouted, 'And that we will be unable to speak to you all individually tonight.'

'It's all right,' Barrett called from his seat in one of the plush boxes flanking stalls and stage. 'They can hear you.'

Best nodded his thanks. Feeling even more foolish, he cleared his throat and continued, 'So, please, if any of you saw anything which you think might be important or you knew the victim, Mr Talisman . . .'

The handsome stained-glass doors to the left of the auditorium swung open, revealing, to Best's relief, two familiar figures: Detective Sergeant Second Class John George Smith and Detective Inspector First Class John George Littlechild. '. . . please speak to me or to these two gentlemen – ' he pointed beyond his audience – 'before you leave.'

They all turned to look at the Scotland Yard detectives now proceeding down the central aisle. Littlechild tipped his hat to them in rakish salute. He should be up here, Best thought.

'We will see the rest of you back here tomorrow at the rehearsal when there will be more officers present. Meanwhile,' he added, voicing a forlorn hope, 'I ask you not to discuss the matter between yourselves.'

As the actors began to disperse, chattering tiredly, Littlechild and Smith came up on to the stage.

'This is some theatre,' murmured Littlechild, pulling at the little pointed tuft of hair beneath his bottom lip and gazing about him in awe. It certainly was. A gilded pleasure dome.

The walls were covered in a rich crimson flock, the seats, cushioned in dark maroon, were of the latest tip-up design while the three gilded tiers of boxes were hung about with deep-crimson silk tapestry lined with Renaissance greens and golds, giving them the look of precious jewel caskets or harem hideaways. The same greens and golds were echoed in the curlicue patterns of the ceiling.

Adding to the impression of decadent splendour was the faint musky odour still hanging in the air as the result of much wafting of the Rimmel-scented stalls theatre programmes.

It was all, thought Best, a very far cry from the Borough Market on a Saturday night.

He was not surprised that Littlechild had been one of the first Scotland Yard detectives to arrive. Best suspected that the man received messages through the ether telling him when a theatrical case was in progress.

Littlechild had a passion for the theatre and music. Not only did he lend his fine tenor voice to the Metropolitan Police Minstrels, who performed to raise funds for the police orphanage, but he was involved in amateur dramatics.

He also delighted in what he called 'the art of disguise'. To the disapproval of his chief and some of his colleagues, he would, at any opportunity, don a butcher's smock and apron and carry a steel or wear an appropriately badged cabman's long coat, drape a horsecloth over his arm and carry a whip in his hand.

'I was kept late with a prisoner,' said Smith, who was less

24

susceptible to the lure of theatre but would go anywhere to help Best, 'so I was still at the office when your message came in.'

Best had known Smith's late father and had got the young man the job as a detective. Since then, they had shared several triumphs and a few terrible tragedies.

'You got your man, then?' Best smiled. 'Well done.'

Smith had been struggling to come to grips with his first long-term fraud case and they were always difficult.

He grinned boyishly, absurdly pleased at the praise.

Two of the supernumeraries were hovering in the wings. Best took one of them aside, a nervous young woman; Smith took the other.

'Wander around, John,' Best said to Littlechild. 'See what you can pick up.'

'Righto!' he replied with enthusiasm.

Best liked the fact that despite being in his fourteenth year of service, Littlechild was ever keen and willing. By then, some of his colleagues had become very blasé and lazy and others found his boundless enthusiasm a little embarrassing.

The young woman's name was Eliza Clark. She'd played an apple seller, Best recalled.

She was about nineteen years old, Best speculated, and small, fair, and plump. Not vastly plump, just pleasantly cushioned all over from her chubby pink cheeks and rounded body to her little, dimpled hands with their tiny, softly padded fingers – resembling those of child's baby doll.

'I didn't *really* know him,' Eliza confessed hurriedly, looking from side to side lest they were overheard, 'but I did talk to him for a little while yesterday.'

'And how did he seem?'

'Upset.' She hesitated then corrected herself. 'At least that's how he seemed to me but of course I didn't know him, so can't be sure. He was sitting by himself on the edge of the stage,' she explained, 'and looked sad. So I went to talk to him.'

'What was he upset about?'

She shook her head, pushing a stray fair strand of hair behind her ear. 'I don't know. I didn't like to pry. At first he

25

just insisted that he was all right. But then we got talking and he was just beginning to tell me what it was when we were called back on stage.'

'What did he *start* to tell you?'

She pursed her rosebud lips and looked apologetic. 'Nothing much. He just said, "It's the others, you know." '

'Did you understand what he meant?'

She shrugged and looked around her. 'Maybe the rest of the cast. Or just the other supers,' she sighed. 'Or maybe he was just . . . a bit, you know.'

She put her right forefinger to her temple and made the screwing movement that, the world over, stands for 'mad'.

'That's all,' she said, embarrassed. 'Sorry . . .'

'No. No. You've been very helpful,' said Best gently. 'You were right to come and tell us.'

So, 'It's the others.'

What on earth could that mean?

Well, at least it was a start.

Seven

Best strode along New Oxford Street, gratefully inhaling the damp, sharpening autumn air. Such a relief after the stuffy, gas-ridden theatre.

He turned into Bloomsbury Street, crossed Great Russell Street and walked up to the elegantly Georgian Bedford Square, which had been christened Judge-land due to the numbers of Her Majesty's judiciary who lived here.

It was a sunny morning and the trees in the square's central oval were alight with autumn's blazing reds and golds. The stuccoed and pilastered fronts of the central houses on each side of the square gleamed white against their plainer brick neighbours. A thin spiral of smoke issued from beside the gardener's hut, sending the sweetly acrid smell of burning leaves across the square.

An anxious driver was giving a final rub to the already gleaming brasses and the shiny black paintwork on a Victoria carriage while trying to keep an eye on one of the front doors at the same time. Either he had had a late night or his mistress had an eagle eye for a speck of dirt.

Looking about him, Best had to admit that the generations of Russells had created a very pleasant area. Well-laid-out streets, handsome great houses and numerous spacious squares. Gates and portentous beadles saved the inhabitants from the nuisances of through traffic and the attentions of beggars, street musicians, hawkers or pedlars. Even tradesmen were not allowed to send their delivery boys into the estate but had to attend in person.

The Russell family – the Dukes and Earls of Bedford and Marquises of Tavistock who had married Gowers and Malets and Torringtons – were all commemorated by these streets and squares.

At the top of the square Best turned right into Montague Place. Situated close to Theatreland, Bloomsbury had also long been the haunt of actors, writers and musicians.

Actors had always tended to gather together. Social lives constrained by their working hours and their low social standing had kept their world small – but that was changing now.

When omnibuses and trains had arrived, a move outwards to leafier spots had begun. Many of the actors moved to Brompton and Bedford Park and, later, Chelsea, Chiswick, Dulwich – even as far afield as Barnes.

Recently, however, a reverse trend had begun – a movement back into town facilitated by the new purpose-built apartment blocks and the dividing off of some of the larger houses into flats.

For the more affluent actors, living near the theatre, at least during the week, was now seen as convenient. Consequently, Central London rents had increased, so, from being the place for all actors, Bloomsbury was becoming colonized by those at the top of their profession. Minor actors, utilities and certainly supers were obliged to find homes further afield among the cheaper brick terraces of Brixton, Clapham, Whitechapel and Shoreditch.

All of which made it something of a surprise that a low-ranking super like Talisman was living in Bloomsbury. Was he really a toff who didn't need to work? Supers' pay was so low that most supers had other jobs. Or was he doing what so many actors did, sharing a house or living in a low-priced boarding house?

Best turned right again into Montague Street, which ran down the eastern side of the British Museum.

The house he was looking for was at the north end.

Like those in Bedford Square, the terraces of Montague Street were built of yellow/brown London brick and, similarly, were five storeys high but of much more modest dimensions than those in London's grandest square. They did not boast massive chequered arched doorways punctuated by sombre Greek philosopher keystones.

Nevertheless, as with much everyday domestic Georgian housing, that of Montague Street had a certain grace and assurance. A certain dignity. In this case, the dignity was somewhat compromised by the large board fixed to the railings announcing in large black letters on a white ground:

KEAN HOUSE
Moderate Terms
Full or Partial Board
Theatricals welcome
Prop: Mrs Elsie Hodgson

The middle-aged woman who answered the door was tiny, with alert blue eyes in a heart-shaped face that retained some remnants of past prettiness. A Christmas tree fairy, past her best but not yet ready to be placed back in the box and forgotten.

She looked him up and down and, clearly taking this well-turned-out gentleman for an actor, said, not impolitely, 'Sorry, dear, we're full up.'

She began closing the door but Best put up his right hand

and waved it back and forth. 'I'm not looking for digs.'

'What then?' she said distractedly. A maid was hovering behind her. The woman turned her head and pointed to the front room and said, 'Needs a good tidy and clean up in there.' She sighed. 'They stayed up very late again and made a terrible mess.'

She turned back to Best. 'I'm not buying anything.'

'I'm not selling anything,' he retorted with a half-smile. He got out his warrant card and held it up. 'I'm a police officer: Detective Inspector Ernest Best.'

'Oh.'

He had her full attention now. She stepped back a little to get a better look at him. 'You could be one of us, you know.'

He grinned. 'So my wife tells me.' He hesitated, adopted a more serious expression and began, 'The reason I am here is . . .'

'It's about Bert Talisman!' she exclaimed. 'Isn't it?'

He nodded.

Now she was transfixed.

Most people were when they found themselves at the heart of a real drama, even actors – especially actors. He hoped she wouldn't react in the tiresome manner of some of the cast of *Lights o' London*, who had launched into performances of 'the vital witness' or 'the innocently accused'.

Mrs Hodgson, however, had clearly been out in the real world long enough to shake off the excesses of her profession.

'I've just heard about it,' she said. 'Terrible business. Who would have wanted to kill that poor, sad, man?'

That poor, sad, man? Interesting.

'That's what we want to find out, Mrs – Mrs Hodgson?'

She inclined her neat little head. 'Yes.' She moved backwards into the dark hall. 'Come in. Come in,' she said. 'Don't know as I can help you – but I'll certainly do my best.'

Mrs Hodgson was correct in her presumption that she might not be able to help. Albert Talisman, it seemed, was determined to remain anonymous even in death.

He had been staying at Kean House for only five nights – one more than his engagement at the Princess's Theatre,

29

having taken residence the day before his first performance.

'Did he say where he had lived before?'

She shook her head. 'Didn't say anything much at all.'

'And you didn't ask him for a reference?'

'He paid the first week in advance.'

Ah, he'd spoken the language of money.

'Was he friendly with any of the other guests?'

'No.' She was unequivocal. 'Not that I saw, anyway.'

'Not even at mealtimes?'

'He didn't come down to meals.'

Best looked at her from under quizzical brows. 'That's unusual. Not even for breakfast?'

'No.'

She smiled her pixie-like smile at his confusion. 'Never been asked to take meals to rooms before. It was a special arrangement. He paid me extra for the service.'

'I see.'

He didn't really.

This was surely odd behaviour for someone in this gregarious profession whose participants, in Best's experience, usually clung together.

It was as if the man wanted to become invisible, untraceable. Like a spy? Or an incognito policeman? That was a thought. He'd know if it was anyone from the Yard but he'd better check with the divisions – they got up to some odd things sometimes.

This whole business was becoming unreal. It had started with a play featuring pretend policemen, gone on to a real murder committed on stage in the middle of the drama and now the victim seemed to have planned to remain anonymous. Even the name – Talisman – was strange. The word meant to be something with a magical power to protect. Well, it hadn't protected its owner.

Best didn't expect to get a helpful reply to his next question but asked it anyway.

'What was Mr Talisman like?'

He was not surprised when his ageing fairy said bluntly, 'I don't know.'

Then she frowned and looked almost guilty as if she felt

the man deserved a fuller epitaph. She took a deep breath and added, 'Well, quiet of course and – sort of sad.'

There was only space enough in Albert Talisman's small and narrow room for the minimum of furniture: a single iron bedstead, a hard upright chair, a plain bedside cabinet, a small wardrobe and a washstand.

The bedhead was pushed up against the outer wall beside a long window that overlooked the southern edge of Russell Square. Above it, attached to the wall, was a bronzed-iron gas lamp with an opal globe and curlicue brackets.

The only picture on the wall, a small T. H. Shepherd print of a London square, was swamped by the pale-brown wall-paper with its black repeating pattern of arches, under which milkmaids dallied and trellises were intertwined with leaves and flowers.

'Plain but comfortable,' said Mrs Hodgson, 'and, as you see, with Venetians and gas laid on.'

Best nodded his approval even though he was always bemused by the way these attractions were so often boasted of in lodging-house advertisements along with 'suitable for a gentleman'.

As though reading his mind Mrs Hodgson pointed to the blinds and explained, 'You can get the light *and* the privacy at the same time.'

A full water jug and glass sat on top of the bedside cabinet. Inside was a fawn canvas wash-roll containing a flannel, shaving soap and brush. Talisman's razor still rested in its cardboard box beside a bottle of Macassar oil and a small wooden box with a brass lock. Ah, now that looked more promising. But where was the key?

He didn't need one. The box wasn't locked. He pulled up the solitary chair, sat down and emptied the contents on to the bed.

The jumble which lay there was made up of a hardback notebook, a postcard-size print of a Hogarth painting, a cheap hairbrush, a gold-coloured locket of half a heart, a pen, pencil, an envelope addressed to Talisman at Kean House, a cheap tin clock and a small, round, shiny pebble.

To the right of the door opposite the window was a

31

washstand and a small, plain oak wardrobe. Hanging inside, they found a pair of black, woollen trousers and a knee-length brown overcoat in the German style – plain and unwaisted with a wide collar and small revers. They were neither shabby nor new but somewhere in between.

On the floor of the wardrobe stood a pair of well-polished black, horse-skin, side-sprung boots, also halfway between new and old.

Best felt about in the large, low patch pocket of the over-coat but it proved to be empty as did the ticket pocket beside the coat edges at waist level.

Best sighed.

Surely there had been more to Albert Talisman's life than this?

Eight

It became clear to Best that he was not going to learn anything new about Talisman from Mrs Hodgson. But that she might be able to extend his knowledge of the Princess's Theatre. He needed to learn as much as he could before bearding the actors and backstage staff again.

In the closed world of acting the latest news and gossip ran as fast as butter over hot crumpets, so, when Talisman's land-lady offered him a cup of coffee, he allowed himself to be persuaded.

He knew it would be an exchange. She was itching to hear the grizzly details of her late boarder's death. He couldn't add much to what she had doubtless already heard but he could dramatize the scene a little and offer Mrs Hodgson an apparently exclusive inside view. After all, the Press had already revealed that the man had been shot in the head while on stage, so it was all going to be in the telling and Helen had assured him that he could tell a good tale.

They sat in the landlady's cosy parlour, which, in contrast to the bareness of her lodgers' rooms, was stuffed with furniture and ornaments. After the tutting and exclamations of horror had subsided, a companionable air of shared experience settled over the pair.

Best ventured mildly, 'A pity that it should happen in what seems to me to be such a well-run theatre.'

He knew she would want to correct him on that. But only after a few complimentary words about the Princess's so as to show loyalty to the profession.

'Oh, yes. Barrett is a marvellous manager and that building is splendid.'

Best nodded his assent.

'Mind you,' she went on, 'the new place struggled a bit before this production. People seemed to find that huge auditorium rather forbidding and stuck up there in Oxford Street on the far fringe of Theatreland. But, this latest production . . .' She spread her small hands wide.

'A triumph.'

'Absolutely.'

There was a short silence before she murmured, 'Actor-manager of course.'

He grimaced knowingly and inclined his head but forbore to comment.

The drawbacks of actor-managers were grumbled about continuously in green rooms and the bars frequented by theatricals – but not within their earshot of course. They held so much power and one might be desperate for a job from them one day. Naturally this lack of criticism to their faces had led actor-managers, as with mighty Roman emperors and the likes of Napoleon, to become unaware of their own foibles or put any hint of them down to jealousy or, as their power grew, not to care too much about the reasons.

The complaints about the worst of them included refusing to employ other talented or promising actors who might become rivals attracting better reviews and more public adoration than they; selecting only plays in which they, themselves, might shine; cutting about the texts of those they did choose so as to enlarge their own roles – and saving money by paying poor wages so they could decorate the sets excessively.

The antics of the worst of them when actually on stage were reputed to be even more reprehensible and spoke of a great meanness of spirit. Ploys such as plain old upstaging; fidgeting while others spoke; jumping in on the speeches of fellow thespians before they had finished and even inducing other actors to speak their lines faster so that they might make use of the time thus saved by slowly declaiming their own to better effect.

Even the lighting could be utilized to add to their greater glorification by arranging it so they were bathed in a wide and golden glow while those sharing the stage disappeared into a stygian gloom.

In rehearsal, they could be so concerned with their own performances that they left the rest of the cast to struggle alone – offering little or no advice from their own rich fund of experience.

Held to be most lethal was their habit of employing members of their own families, whether suitable for the stage or not. Thus, at one stroke, they denied work to more qualified actors and lowered the status of the profession.

Their defenders pointed out that actor-managers were a necessity. The theatre needed their drive, power, connections and popularity. Wasn't it they whom audiences flocked to see? All were star performers – the public's darlings who could do no wrong.

To the suggestion that Britain might instead have state subsidized theatre like France and Germany these defenders responded by exclaiming about the British loving their freedom too much to be dictated to by the state. It was what had made us great.

Some freedom, shouted the anti-actor-managers, when they have us in a stranglehold!

And so it went on.

Best had heard the arguments from Littlechild. Mrs Hodgson knew them from long experience.

'But, as they go,' Mrs Hodgson said, 'I hear that Mr Wilson

Barrett is better than most. Less selfish and kinder.' She smiled. 'A little vain, perhaps . . .' Best smiled back. They both knew of his reputation for wearing unnecessarily décolleté costumes to show off his manly chest. 'But I don't think you'll find much simmering resentment if that's what you're looking for.'

He was. Well, in a manner of speaking.

Chances were that the death of the mysterious Mr Albert George Talisman was an entirely personal matter but you could never be sure at this stage. Best knew from his experience that some people had an amazing inclination towards simmering resentment. They hugged it to themselves. It gave them a purpose in life.

Harming the theatre or the play could be a motive. Certainly the Lord Chamberlain would be wanting to know why a real gun loaded with real bullets came to be on stage. He might even close them down.

They smiled at each other. She was his match.

'But theatres all have their problems, don't they?' He took another sip of her excellent coffee. 'Little scandals and accidents and squabbles.'

'Y-e-s. I can't think of anything recent at the Princess's but then – ' she sighed – 'I'm not privy to the daily happenings now. Of course they've had problems with fire.'

'Don't they all,' Best responded.

'The Park,' she said, shaking her head.

'Terrible, that.'

Indeed, on the very opening night of *The Lights o' London* at the Princess's, The Park Theatre in Camden Town had been totally destroyed by fire. Fortunately, the conflagration had broken out at around midnight, well after the audience and all the employees had left.

That very evening they had been scheduled to open with two new productions. A new comedy, *Marriage Bells,* and the popular drama *Delilah.*

Would they have provided unwanted competition for the just launched *Lights o' London* at a theatre which up to then had been struggling? As far as Best knew, no one had considered that possibility at the time.

'The really bad fire at the Princess's was that terrible one with the dancers but – ' she shook her head – 'that was way back.'

Best watched with fascination as she held on to and shook her tiny little finger to emphasize her point, then progressed to the next small digit to emphasize another.

'There *was* that scandal when the dresser was arrested.'

Ah yes. Best remembered that one. The man, Thomas Harris, a dresser to the principals, had been caught accidentally when the management had called in the police to investigate thieving from the dressing rooms.

When Harris was searched on leaving the theatre, remnants of soap, a towel and stage money were found on him.

'But that was two or three years ago in the old theatre.'

Best got the feeling she was throwing him some obvious possibilities to keep him from discovering something more pertinent. Now why would she do that?

Harris had got away with it, Best recalled, after the actor, William Terriss, a kindly man, had spoken up for him and his defence had claimed that soap remnants were widely regarded as a dresser's perquisites. It was decided that the prosecution was a paltry one and the case was dismissed. Best had been more curious about what the man had intended to do with that fake money.

'What happened to him?'

'I don't know,' Mrs Hodgson shrugged. 'Just after the case he wrote a rather pathetic letter to *The Era*. It was rather peculiar. He described his career as a dresser and his poor health and so on but didn't say anything about the charge, simply calling it his fall from grace. I wondered what the point of it all was.'

The Era was a leading theatrical publication. Maybe he had been hoping to elicit sympathy and thus gain work?

Best made a mental note to find out what had happened to dresser Thomas Harris after his fall from grace.

Helen was not so impressed by the notion of Wilson Barrett as one of the few democratic and unselfish actor-managers.

'As far as the male actors, maybe,' she pointed out, 'but

not the women. With them, he's just the same as all the rest.'

Best didn't say anything. He knew she had been upset by her meeting with the crushed Mary Eastlake.

'They're all the same. Look at that Henry Irving – making his Shylock so dignified and heroic and aristocratic that Ellen Terry's Portia – one of the few meaty parts for women – merely seemed small and petty and spiteful. Totally ruined her trial scene. Hah!'

As she spoke her brush strokes – usually so controlled and careful – had become angry stabs and thrusts as though the offending males were there before her on the canvas.

'Careful, dearest,' he ventured, 'or you'll ruin St Nicholas's Church and you wouldn't want that, would you?'

She glared at him.

'After all,' he went on recklessly, 'it's where you saved the life of this poor, wretched, undeserving male.' He sighed dramatically.

She narrowed her eyes at him and he affected a drooping, put-down stance which caused her to begin tutting, glancing skywards in disgust and exclaiming 'Huh! Huh!'

When she looked at him again he was dabbing his eyes and adopting a sad puppy expression. Her mouth began to twitch.

'Ernest Best! I'm serious!'

'So am I, my beloved.'

She threw down her brush, strode over to where he was sitting on a chair alongside the wall of her studio, grabbed him by the chin and kissed him hard on the mouth.

'You don't deserve a good and obedient wife like me.'

'I know,' he sighed again, standing up and grabbing her around the waist. 'But I only wish I had one.'

They both laughed and held each other very tight. She really *had* saved his life after he had been sent north to Newcastle upon Tyne to assist the local police with a difficult case.

Not only had he just lost his young fiancée but he blamed himself for not preventing the murder of one of the northern town's policemen and a local barmaid. He was at his lowest ebb when Helen had miraculously appeared, having been commissioned to draw Britain's latest cathedral. She'd pulled him up again and, at last, accepted him.

They looked at the painting, remembered and clung even more tightly to each other until she said, 'No, dear. Not here, just now, I'm expecting a visitor.'

She wiped the paint from her hands in a businesslike fashion and said, 'Now, tell me what you've discovered so far?'

Nine

Best tipped out the contents of the pillowcase which contained Albert Talisman's few personal possessions.

'There ain't much, is there,' said Smith sadly as they began to examine them in the hope that they might provide inspiration or maybe a tiny clue as to the man's identity.

'No. In fact I didn't want to take the stuff. I'd looked it over and noted everything, so didn't see the point.' He lifted his shoulders. 'But Mrs Hodgson insisted. Said it didn't belong to her.'

'I expect she wants to let the room again as soon as possible.'

He picked up the divided heart necklace and held it up to the light. 'A memento of a lady, I expect. A girlfriend or maybe his mother. It don't look like it's worth much.'

Best was surprised to see the small picture from Talisman's wall was among the objects. He hadn't noted that down, thinking it part of the furnishings of Mrs Hodgson's 'simple but comfortable' room where it had been drowned in a mélange of trellises and milkmaids.

About twelve inches by nine, framed in well-worn pale wood, it was a typical T. H. Shepherd print of a noted London scene of the 1820s–30s.

In the foreground were the usual Regency figures: gentlemen in tight white breeches and bucket-shaped tall black hats and ladies in their high-waisted gowns and demure bonnets. There was a coach or gig or two and some of the gentlemen were on horseback.

All were incidental to, a mere dressing for, the background, which, in this case, was Brunswick Square in St Pancras – no distance from Talisman's lodgings.

'Suggests he might have been a local man,' he murmured, 'but then again it might not.' He sighed. 'Who knows?'

'Might just be a present,' said Smith. He knew that Best could become depressed when a case went up a blind alley and this one didn't seem to do much else. 'But – but that might mean something as well.'

'I suppose we ought to look around the square to see if anyone knows him.' He thought of all those witnesses at the theatre whose statements had to be sifted. 'When we get time, that is. If we get time.'

He turned his attention to the Hogarth print which was entitled *The March to Finchley*.

Like much of Hogarth's work it wasn't exactly complimentary to its subject. In this instance, the painting showed the King's drunken and bedraggled guards as they passed the Tottenham Court turnpike. They were supposedly off to Finchley Common to take part in army manoeuvres but were dallying en route, to say the least, with a rabble of prostitutes and other camp followers.

What a strange picture to have among your belongings.

'Them bruises ain't new,' announced Detective Chief Inspector Cheadle. 'The surgeon says they was done a few days before – or some of them was anyway.'

The old boy sat in Wilson Barrett's office looking like a truculent walrus.

He needn't have turned up at the theatre to tell Best that but he just couldn't help poking his nose in, particularly now he was finally on the road to retirement. Only a combination of progressively less gentle hints from his superiors combined with the not inconsequential insistence of Mrs Cheadle were at last bringing this about.

In one sense the big man would be a great loss to the department. His nose for villains and villainy was still unerring but his age was beginning to tell in respects such as a lack of concentration and a tendency to fall asleep at inopportune moments.

The realization that something must be done about him came when he actually nodded off at one of Sir Howard Vincent's conferences. Only a stiffening of Chief Superintendent Williamson's shoulder and a dig in Cheadle's ribs had stopped him falling over.

The Director of the CID held his conferences at his desk with his Yard detectives standing ranged around him in a respectful semicircle.

'Like 'e was the Queen, or some sultan or something,' Cheadle had been heard to mutter.

Unlike some ageing men, Cheadle was becoming more benign as the years rolled by. Best reckoned this was because the man had already used up his ration of irascibility. But the acid still leaked out now and then and he did become a little truculent if he felt he was being left out of things.

That said, Best was relieved that at least not much venom was directed in his direction these days. I've become one of the old school now, he realized, not a cocky youngster to be kept in my place.

'Well, what's the picture, then?' Cheadle demanded. 'Who's this bloke Talisman?'

If only we knew, thought Best. But he painted the scene as well as he could, given the sparsity of materials.

'Hmm,' said Cheadle. He patted the elaborately carved pseudo-George III mahogany chair on which he sat and glanced around at the unaccustomed comfort of his surroundings. 'Do themselves all right these theatricals, don't they?'

'Some do,' admitted Best. 'Others get a pittance.'

He wasn't there to discuss the relative comfort of the lives of others. The old boy really was getting senile.

'Might be some resentment there, then,' Cheadle warned. 'People gets very bitter about money.' He pushed his huge body upright in the mahogany chair after it had done its usual trick of slipping down.

They both had experience of such jealousy. One of Vincent's first actions when he took office after the branch's

40

corruption scandal had been to raise the salaries of the detectives – to the fury of the uniform branch.

But Best couldn't see how financial envy could be a factor in this case unless Talisman was getting some money from another source. Perhaps he belonged to a wealthy family and someone resented the fact? Perhaps Cheadle wasn't so senile after all?

'I was just off to find out the result of all those interviews with the audience and the actors and—'

'Don't do that,' Cheadle interrupted as Best began to move towards the door. He *had* to do that next. If he didn't he'd lose his grip on the inquiry!

'Go and see that Super Master again. 'E must know 'ow 'e came in contact with Talisman. If it ain't come to 'im yet – lean on 'im.'

Cheadle was a great leaner.

Best could also lean on reluctant witnesses when pushed but he preferred to acquire his knowledge in a more subtle and civilized manner.

Nonetheless, if he were pushed or unduly irritated or stonewalled he could lean with the best of them. But to do that he needed a lever. Something with which to frighten a witness. Hold over them. As far as Best could see he didn't have that with Harold Smart, the Princess's Super Master.

The sight of the man with his clipboard and supercilious expression engendered sufficient irritation to send Best into a more leaning mood. He just didn't have time to resume the dance around this man.

'You again,' said Smart ungraciously as Best approached. 'Told you all I know before.' He tapped a stringy finger on his clipboard. 'And I'm busy just now.'

Best was all imperturbability. 'Ah, but you may have information, valuable information, of which you are unaware.'

Had he known Best better, Smart would have recognized the danger signs in the careful, pedantic enunciation. But he didn't.

'Doubt it,' he said, turning away rudely.

41

'Let's just see, shall we,' cajoled Best but with a hint of steel creeping into his voice.

'Ain't got time,' said Smart dismissively but with a little less certainty in his. 'Got to find a replacement for Talisman and they're starting to do call-ins for the next production.'

'Won't take a minute,' insisted Best.

'No,' said Smart.

'Oh, very well.' Best sighed and began to turn away. 'I'll just tell Mr Barrett that you refuse to co-operate with me and therefore we are obliged to close the theatre down.'

'Here – just a minute!'

'That's all I want, Mr Smart. A minute. I would imagine,' he went on, giving vent to his spleen, 'judging by Mr Barrett's anger when he was unable to find you yesterday evening, he is aware of your problem and already has you on a short leash.'

'What d'you mean, "my problem"?' Smart's gaunt cheeks had gone grey-white and there was real fear in his voice.

'Oh, it's the talk of the Green Room.'

'What is?! What is?!'

'Your addiction to the demon drink, Mr Smart. The way you put alcohol before your work.' Best took a deep breath and went in for the kill. 'What's more, your reluctance to give us a little simple information arouses our suspicions. Makes alarm bells ring in our heads. What could your motive be? What are you hiding, eh?'

'Nothing! Nothing!'

The man was desperate now.

'Reassure me, Mr Smart.'

'What is it? What do you want to know?'

'Where do you get your supers from?'

'Everywhere, everywhere,' he insisted, trying to please. Some comes and sees us when they're doing the rounds, some we 'ad before so know about them, some come to us through agents.'

'Right, so far, so good.' Best paused. 'Now, how did Mr Talisman come to your notice?'

'I told you, we'd had him before.'

'But where, then, had he come from? Was it through an agent by any chance?'

'How would I know?' He was rallying a little.

'You'd know, Mr Smart, because agents charge fees and you'd have that on your records.'

'But I'd have to check back – with the treasurer.'

'Correct. Do that. Your system is in good order, I presume?'

'Yeah, course.'

'Good. And, Mr Smart – ' Best halted the man as he turned to go – 'don't be tempted to fob me off, to just pretend to do a check. If you do, I promise you – ' he slowed down to spell out the words with great emphasis – 'you will regret it – bitterly. Understand?'

The chastened man nodded. 'Yes.'

As Helen often told him, the spectacle of the easy-going Best in high dudgeon was a frightening one.

Ten

There were good theatrical agents and bad theatrical agents. Good agents tried to find their client suitable work like they were supposed to do.

Bad agents either didn't bother whether the role for which they sent them to read was suitable or not, or did not send them to any, merely pocketing their registration fee and then forgetting about them.

Needless to say, these very bad agencies tended to close down suddenly only to re-establish themselves after a short interval under a different name.

Frobishers was one of the better theatrical agents. Best learned this from Rosa de la Drake, the attractive young actress who sat alongside him in its poster-bedecked outer office while they both awaited the arrival of the great man: the agent himself.

Mr Augustus Frobisher held the key, if not to greatness,

then at least to a desperately needed job – if only one could attract and hold his attention in the face of stiff competition.

Rosa, Best also learned, was doing her morning rounds in the hope of landing a principal or semi-principal role. Or, at least, to be taken on as a utility, or hired for one of the forthcoming pantomimes or maybe to do burlesque. Even, at a pinch, in music hall. She could sing and dance a little but didn't really want to go down that path – music hall – lest it blemish her status as a respectable actress.

As she spoke she enunciated her words rather carefully, giving due and undue emphasis to H's and R's and ending her words crisply – most of the time at least. Clearly Rosa had been taking elocution lessons.

She was kindly initiating Best, who had admitted to being a newcomer to the business, into the rigours of 'looking for an engagement'. This, she declared, was quite the nastiest part of theatrical life – at least for small fry like themselves.

'You must start out early,' she explained, 'wearing your best clothes – no matter what the weather.'

A good appearance, she went on, was of course particularly important for ladies.

Well, Rosa had certainly succeeded in that. She had gathered her blue-black hair into a chignon, from which spilled a waterfall of shiny ringlets, then garnished it with a confection of ribbons and feathers.

Her black hair, dark eyes and olive skin gave Rosa a faintly Spanish air. She had emphasized this, he guessed, by intensifying the depth of her hair colour, adopting the exotic name and choosing clothes of a hue she imagined might be worn by a señorita in Andalucia. In this instance, a deep-pink ensemble with blood-red trimmings, earrings and necklace. Even her perfume had a pungent Moorish tinge.

'You have to be different to stand out – but not *too* different,' she advised Best. 'Of course, I have these as well.' She extracted from her bag a folder containing photographs of herself in various guises from daisy-decked fresh English maiden to handsome young man. She pointed to the latter. 'That was my only breeches part so far.'

She looked him over. '*Your* look is quite good. Foreign –

you could play Mediterranean – or an English villain.'

Wait till he told Helen, she would love that!

Rosa had a tiny waist and, judging by the faint creaking sounds as she moved, this was at least partly due to extra-tight lacing. She also rustled. Unlike the creaking, this effect was deliberate.

'It is particularly important for ladies seeking an engagement to wear a silk petticoat,' she revealed gravely. 'A silk petticoat that rustles as she walks.'

Apparently, not only did the petticoat give one confidence, making one feel well-to-do and so not really being desperately in need of work, but it gave others that same impression. Thus, they would offer one only the better, well-paid roles. 'A silk petticoat which rustles and white kid gloves are essential,' she said firmly.

More fascinating insights into other people's lives! He often shared such revelations with Helen, who also delighted in them.

However, he decided that this particular one he would keep to himself. He could just imagine what Helen would say when told about the vital importance to an actress's career of a silk petticoat which rustled and over-tight stays that creaked.

'Then you must smile sweetly and be charming,' Rosa continued, 'even to the rude little office boy behind the desk who shrugs you off when you confess to committing the terrible crime of arriving without an appointment and tells you in a surly manner, "Then you'll just have to wait and see."'

'Wait you do. The room fills up with those blessed with appointments and girls who are much prettier than you. But still you try to keep your spirits up.' As she said that, her voice faltered and she looked away while she composed herself.

Sometimes, she went on, the nasty little office boy would eventually announce, with a smirk on his face, that the agent wasn't coming in that day, after all. Or he might declare that the man's presence was imminent. In this case, one would place oneself by the door in the hope of catching him as he came in . . .

As she spoke, such a message was passed and Rosa de la Drake leaped to her feet, smoothed down her deep rose-coloured gown, pasted on her most comely smile and rustled over to stand just inside the door.

When it opened, a harassed-looking, portly little man came in. His gaze was directed firmly towards his office door at the far side of the room, which he clearly intended to reach unhindered. But Rosa put out her white kid-gloved hand, touched his arm lightly and murmured something to him.

He stopped to listen, head on one side, eyes averted from the rest of the people in the room. Then Best heard him say, 'Nothing today, my dear, but I'm bearing you in mind.' He squeezed her hand. 'Look in again when you are passing.'

And that was that. At least he hadn't been rude. Best didn't think he could have borne it if the man had been rude. He himself was quickly ushered into the agent's office while Rosa de la Drake left to continue her quest for an engagement.

Three large pieces of furniture dominated the office of Augustus Frobisher. To the left of the door was a massive mahogany desk on which were placed a long index box and a few manila files. Over by the window, which looked out over Oxford Street, stood a well-used grand piano, its music stand crammed with popular song sheets.

Leaning against the right-hand wall rested a glossy ebony screen decorated with chrysanthemums, Japanese roses, and oriental gentlemen scurrying across bridges, carrying extraordinarily heavy loads on thin shoulders.

A combination of the businesslike and flamboyant – most appropriate for a man in his profession.

Placed about the room were photographs of well-known actors embellished with inscriptions profuse in their gratitude and, on the wall behind the desk, were two large posters.

The first was a crisp new playbill for *The Lights o' London*. With hand-coloured lithographs it depicted the fight in the Borough and Harold's dramatic rescue of Seth Preene from drowning, a brave feat which induced the man to recover his conscience and determine to save Harold in return.

The second, yellowed and faded with age, listed the scenes

in Boucicault's *The Streets of London,* performed at the old Princess's Theatre way back in 1864. These included the famous fire scene which had caused such a sensation at the time. Obviously, Augustus Frobisher had been doing business with the Princess's Theatre for some time.

Frobisher began by saying how sorry he was to hear of Talisman's death. Unlike some, he refrained from making play of the drama within a drama aspect. Merely remarked, as he placed gold half-spectacles on his nose and withdrew an index card from the section marked 'T', that he would help all he could but had to confess that he didn't really know much about Talisman.

'As you observe – ' he waved his plump, ringed hand towards the outer office – 'I see so many people.'

His job is not unlike mine, Best thought soon after they had begun talking: taking control of the interview, being pleasant but firm when necessary and telling lies or half-truths – for the greater good or out of kindness. Fortunately, lies weren't necessary in this case.

The address he furnished from the card and Talisman's description, his list of talents, and suitability for various roles was identical to that already culled from Smart's supers register.

The man's previous engagements were more of a surprise. He had worked at the Lyceum, the Prince of Wales and, of course, the Princess's. But at the first two he had been employed as an actor – a utility – and had even at one stage understudied one of the principals.

Best was perplexed. 'So, you couldn't get him any more acting work? Was he a drunk or unreliable?'

Drink was the curse of the acting profession and being late for rehearsals or, unforgivably, performances, was one of several ways an actor could earn the deadly 'unreliable' reputation.

'Oh, yes. I could have got him more acting. See here.' Frobisher pointed an immaculately manicured finger halfway down the index card. 'He had another offer – a good offer – from the Bancrofts at the Prince of Wales.' He shook his head wonderingly. 'Many actors would kill to get into that

47

company, but – ' Frobisher extracted his gold half-hunter from his waistcoat pocket, flicked open the lid and glanced at the time – 'suddenly he only wanted to work at the Princess's.'

'Even if it was just as a super?'

'Even if it was just as a super,' Frobisher confirmed.

After a little essential refreshment Best hurried back along the south side of busy Oxford Street in the shade of an avenue of awnings erected by shopkeepers, anxious to prevent even the weak autumn sunshine from fading their goods.

He was anxious to learn what information had been culled from the audience and actors regarding last night's onstage murder. Fortunately, he could discount the members of the orchestra – their eyes would be concentrated on their music or the conductor and their minds on the next intermission and their pint of ale.

He had to admit that, in a sense, Cheadle had been right that the theatrical agent would have interesting information to offer. It *was* very interesting that Talisman was so insistent on working at the Princess's that he would forgo more money and better prospects.

But Best couldn't help thinking that by being absent at this crucial time he was allowing the inquiry to slip out of his hands – always fatal. All those witnesses must have seen something vital.

By Poland Street he stopped to look across the street at the frontage of the new Princess's. Given the massive seating capacity, it was still surprisingly narrow. The width only of one of the smaller shops, it was wedged, like an afterthought, between a ladies' boot-maker and a goldsmith's.

But its emerald-green awning stood out among the sun-bleached blinds of the adjoining properties as did the elongated, Portland stone arch above. This arch cleverly echoed the stage inside by framing a huge window behind which plush red curtains were drawn back.

The unique final touch was the open-air balcony at the foot of the handsome arch. Here, between acts, the occupants of the more expensive seats might enjoy a smoke while absorbing the sights, smells and sounds of a bustling Oxford Street.

It was an extraordinary and much commented-upon innovation. One could not deny, thought Best, that the architect had made the most of a cramped site, giving the impression of a tiny gem inserted among its more crass commercial neighbours.

The heart of one of Europe's busiest shopping streets did seem a rather odd place to have a theatre. Indeed, the premises had once been a bazaar but had been converted into a theatre in 1836 and named after the then Princess Victoria.

When she became Queen, she rewarded them with regular patronage, particularly during the glory days of Charles Kean's management, and bestowed the title Royal upon the theatre.

Optimistic 'BUSINESS AS USUAL' notices were propped up outside the front entrance (intended solely for use of the wealthier patrons) and stood on the marbled mosaic floor of the vestibule.

Hovering anxiously inside, the front-of-house staff were endeavouring to send out the same calm message in answer to enquiries: nothing irredeemably untoward occurred yesterday evening. All is well.

One of them came forward, bowed his stiff-collared neck and murmured discreetly, 'Excuse me, sir. Your colleagues are in the Number One male dressing room on the dress-circle floor.'

Now he was to learn from his police colleagues just how many of the audience of two thousand had witnessed the event. One thing was certain, a great many would claim to have done so. When, as a young uniformed street policeman, Best had enquired of bystanders whether they had seen an accident or attack they would inevitably reply in the affirmative. Equally inevitably it would transpire that they had heard the terrible scream and/or the resounding crash – then turned around to see – the accident or attack.

Very few, he learned by hard experience, had actually seen the pedestrian fall under the wheels of the carriage or the knife slide into a victim's chest. What they had seen was the immediate aftermath while imagining that they had witnessed the whole thing.

As expected, a great many of the audience had witnessed the incident. Or, at least, had noticed the chestnut seller lying on the floor and had realized instantly that something was seriously wrong. Some had even guessed that the man was dead. It was just gut instinct that had told them this.

What they had not witnessed, of course, was the actual shooting. Nor had they noticed who had picked up the gun from where it had fallen and fired it at Talisman's head.

Not unnaturally, most eyes had been fixed on the hero, Harold, and his distraught wife, Bess.

'I didn't want him to be caught, did I!'

'There was such a melee it was not possible to pick one ruffian out from another.' This, from a discerning member of middle classes who were now making up an increasing proportion of the audiences.

'My eyes were on that poor Bess. Did you see how that horrible Clifford threw her aside?'

'He hadn't done nothing, poor fellah. Why'd they 'ave to grab 'im like that!'

. . . and so it went on.

'It was as if they thought it was all *real*,' exclaimed one young constable still green enough to be surprised by the things people did and said.

'He's right!' exclaimed another, shaking his head in wonder. 'You know, at first some of them wouldn't tell us nothing 'cos they thought we was after that fellah what Barrett plays – like we was the same as the stage policemen!'

It hadn't helped that most of the officers had neither seen the play nor had any idea what it was about.

Some of the least gullible observers proved to be those more seasoned playgoers and real aficionados of the drama, the half-pricers and the Dead Heads.

Indeed, it was one of these Dead Heads, Ada Bartram, a plain and hesitant young kitchen maid with a prominent bosom and a pronounced squint in her left eye, who offered the only piece of interesting evidence. Indeed, most peculiar evidence it was too.

'You'll be interested in what this one has to say,' Smith had told him as he ushered Ada into their temporary meeting room.

But, by then, she had become rigid with fright at her sudden emergence into the spotlight. She sat gazing at Best like a rabbit caught in a stoat's thrall – at least her good eye did.

To relax her he leaned forward casually, arms on his knees, hands folded loosely, and began chatting away inconsequentially. Endeavouring to keep his attention fixed on the right eye, he told her how he had been to see the play last night but that, due to the accident, he had not seen the end and couldn't imagine what it could be. Could she?

Her mouth opened and she tried to speak but only a squeak came out.

'But then, you wouldn't know either, would you? Not having seen the end either.' He shrugged apologetically. 'You must think I'm awful worrying about that when . . .'

She was shaking her head.

'I do,' she said suddenly.

'Er, you do . . . ?'

'Know what 'appened next.'

He was puzzled. 'But if you were there last night and—'

'I've seen it before.'

'Oh, I see. But you were there last night?'

'No.'

'I see,' repeated Best, but he didn't.

What was Smith playing at?!

'One of the other times they was hitting him.'

'Er, who was hitting . . . who?'

He scratched his head. Was it the lack of sleep that was making it hard for him to grasp what she was talking about?

'That chestnut seller. The man what got killed. The third night I was here, some of the others were giving him little pushes and punches.'

'Oh.'

Best sat back, relinquishing his casual stance. This *was* interesting!

'Who were hitting him? Which ones?'

She shook her head. 'I can't remember. I wouldn't have even noticed they were doing it because when I'd been before I'd just looked at Harold – Mr Barrett.'

She blushed and Best realized what brought her back night

51

after night to queue in the rain and cold on the chance of a last-minute free ticket: more sightings of the handsome Mr Wilson Barrett who was such a success with the ladies in the audience.

'But, by then, d'you see, I knew Harold wasn't going to get away but that he'd be all right later.' She had found her voice and was in full flow now. 'So, then I began noticing the rest of them – 'ow they pretended to fight and that.'

'Yes, clever, isn't it?'

Best was on the edge of his seat, willing her to remember more.

'An' that's when I noticed that some of them weren't pretending but was really giving that poor man little digs – and you could tell they really hurt 'im.'

'But you can't remember which ones were doing it?'

She bit her lip anxiously. 'No, I'm sorry!'

'Don't worry, don't worry.' He patted her hand. 'It may come back to you later. Even if it doesn't you've been a great help.' He paused. 'But it *was* more than *one* of them?'

'Oh, yes,' she agreed. 'It was different people in the crowd.'

Eleven

B est was uncertain what to do about this new information. Should he approach the supers en masse with the accusation that they had been seen attacking one of their own?

He thought not.

That would forewarn the culprits, who might take further steps to protect themselves by waxing indignant at an attack from an outsider, rally the troops behind them or even resort to intimidation of their colleagues.

What he needed was a spy in the ranks to help him find out what was going on and to discover whether it had anything to do with the subsequent murder.

No use sending in Smith this time.

When they had been up in Newcastle upon Tyne Smith had made a splendid drapery assistant.

But in any case he was tall and strapping while most actors, Best had noticed, tended to be short and slight. Also, Smith's boyishly handsome face and tall frame was already familiar to several of the cast, particularly the ladies.

Given his experience, Littlechild would be most suited to playing a walk-on thespian but, again, his presence had been well noted and Best doubted whether any of the man's ingenious disguises would fool the professionals. Besides, he couldn't see the ebullient Littlechild taking a modest back seat as a super, particularly after his leading roles with the Metropolitan Police Minstrels.

Eventually, Best decided that he would put this new information to one side for the moment. He'd learned from bitter experience that it was sometimes better to hold fire rather than rush into something just for the sake of feeling you must do something or be seen to take action.

Meanwhile, he would correct an oversight he'd been guilty of in one of his previous actions.

It had dawned on him that, as Talisman had only recently moved to Kean House, there must have been other addresses on his index card at the agency. Doubtless these had been crossed out but not, he hoped, too heavily. Therefore, he would go back to Frobisher's, taking Smith with him, and ask to see the card.

Pity he wouldn't meet Rosa this time. She might have been able to tell him why supers would turn against one of their own.

Maybe the agency would give him her address? But would his motives be misconstrued? They might imagine that he too thought actresses were no better than prostitutes. He would not ask for Rosa's address lest he besmirched her reputation. As she had pointed out to him in her treatise on the vagaries of the acting world: an actress's reputation is the most precious thing she owns.

Now it was no longer thronged with eager actors and actresses the outer office of Frobisher's Theatrical Agency looked quite different. You could see that the furniture was quite old, scuffed and shabby and the carpet was well worn.

Despite the playbills lining the yellowing walls, the room had a forlorn air as if haunted by the dashed dreams of so many hopefuls.

'He's just leavin',' said the surly office boy, obviously thinking Best was after one of those Mediterranean roles, 'and we're shut.'

'Tell him,' said Best crisply, flicking open his warrant card and thrusting it under the boy's nose, 'that it's Detective Inspector Best and Detective Sergeant Smith of Scotland Yard and that it's urgent.'

The lad's eyes widened. Scotland Yard detective! 'Oh yes, sir. Certainly, sir.'

'I won't keep him long.'

The boy scuttled off.

He was soon back.

'He'll only be a few minutes, sir.'

He hovered, gazing up at Best with an eager expression on his pert and spotty face. Best knew that he was dying to hear tales about coiners, thieves and murderers, and the exciting life of a Scotland Yard detective. But he ignored the little bully.

Instead, he took the opportunity to peruse the playbills.

'I didn't get a chance to look at them earlier,' he explained to Smith. 'The room was so full and I was chatting with Rosa.'

'Rosa?' Smith raised his eyebrows.

'Don't look like that!' Best laughed. 'She was giving me lessons in how to get acting work and I reckon we need to learn all we can about this business. Apparently it can be a hard life for those starting out.'

He ignored Smith's smirks and turned his attention back to the playbills.

A dog-eared one announced the final production at the Princess's of actor-manager Charles Keane's *Henry VIII*.

Kean was renowned for ensuring that the scenery and costumes for his Shakespeare 'revivals' were as authentic as possible. This passion of his had earned his productions the epithet 'archaeological'. In other words he dug up the correct information.

So it came as no surprise that the scenery for his *Henry VIII* was allotted as much space as the cast and there were even source notes beside many of the sets verifying their authenticity such as: 'Room in the Palace of Bridewell. Introducing a chimney piece, designed by Holbein for this Palace, from a drawing in the British Museum.'

Next to that was a cartoon on the subject of the spanking new Gilbert & Sullivan forthcoming production of *Patience* at the new Savoy Theatre. It showed long-haired male aesthetes wearing knee-breeches while consorting with their lady counterparts in loose 'Renaissance' gowns with uncommonly large and puffed-up sleeves.

But what interested Best most was another old playbill for that extraordinary 'sensational drama' *It's Never Too Late to Mend,* which had been staged at the old Princess's in 1865. It had been a world away from Kean's classical revivals.

'That caused such a sensation when it opened,' Best told Smith who must have been about ten years old at the time. 'The scenes of prison life were too realistic for some. You wouldn't believe the uproar they caused.'

Best himself had been only about nineteen when he had gazed down on them from the old Princess's gallery. They had shown it all: the treadmill, prisoners picking oakum till their fingers bled, brutal warders and the worst horrors of the separate and silent system, demonstrated by lines of hooded inmates.

But what had given the melodrama such a sensational reputation was the reaction of the first-night audience to the flogging of the young prisoner Josephs, who had been played by Miss Louisa Moore.

'There was such an uproar and even shouts of "Revolting!" from one of the critics! The actor-manager, George Vining, had to step out of his own role as another prisoner and address the audience.

'He explained that they weren't trying to be sensational,' Best went on. 'That it was a serious piece and he pointed out the good that had already been done by the original book. But – ' Best smiled – 'they did tone down that scene and another in which Josephs attempted suicide.'

The furore hadn't done the play any harm, Best remembered. Indeed, the publicity obviously whetted many and various appetites because it went on to quite a long run to packed houses.

'There were some amazing sets.' Best pointed to 'The Programme of Scenery'.

The largest and the boldest amongst the wild mixture of typefaces was kept for the most sensational or heart-rending scenes:

TREADMILL
CORRIDORS
LOG HUT IN AUSTRALIA
A RAVINE: THE GREAT NUGGET!!!
HOME AGAIN.

'CORRIDORS' might not have sounded very dramatic but it was the one that stayed in the young Best's mind. It showed gloomy, cell-flanked passages and corridors receding into the distance, joined at intervals by huge, iron staircases from which further cell-lined passages radiated in the fashion of a spider's web.

'Later, when I went to Pentonville to inspect the prisoner releases, I realized it had been used as a model for the set.'

'That book did help change things in prisons, you know,' said Augustus Frobisher, coming up behind them in a waft of citrus cologne.

The powerful agent was resplendent in an elegant evening tailcoat with a quilted collar and a white silk waistcoat. His manner was more relaxed than on Best's previous visit but his eyes more tired.

'I saw it when Ida Blackmore stood in for Louisa Moore as the boy Josephs,' said Best. In fact, he'd been rather taken with Ida and certain she was heading for great things. 'Whatever happened to her?'

Frobisher grimaced and shook his head. 'I have no idea. She failed to turn up for a performance one evening and never bothered to explain why. Of course, once she'd done that there was little chance of getting back – and she'd know that.' He

56

shrugged. 'Sad, I had high hopes for that young lady.'

'So did I.' Best smiled ruefully.

His hunch about Talisman's previous addresses proved to be correct. There were two more – crossed out but decipherable. Both of them were in Bloomsbury.

He took one and handed the other to Smith saying, 'I'll see you afterwards in the Bodega Bar in Bedford Street.'

The Bodega Bar was the area's favourite theatrical public house. 'With luck we'll bump into someone who knew our victim.'

One person who had witnessed the flogging of the boy prisoner on stage that night felt it was no more than he/she deserved. Indeed, thought that it ought to have been a real thrashing – performed by him.

Ida had disappointed him.

Mortally offended him, in fact.

He had watched her become a ladylike young super then go on to flower in utility roles as an obedient serving maid or a kindly sister.

But now – this! How dare she!

He had warned her not to take the part. But she had defied him. Claimed that this was her great opportunity.

More like a descent into degradation.

Twelve

'You know what I think?' enquired Helen, asking one of those questions she didn't expect him to answer. '*I* think that Talisman was an orphan who lived at the Foundling Hospital in Coram's Fields.'

Best was startled.

'Whatever makes you—'

'It's obvious,' she interrupted, pointing to the picture of Brunswick Square among the victim's belongings. 'That square adjoins the Fields, doesn't it? And what's more,' she added triumphantly, 'the original painting of that Hogarth print is in the secretary's office at the hospital.'

Helen had some knowledge of the subject. She had drawn the scene at the viewing mornings held in the dining room of the orphanage. These were occasions when the rich and fashionable were given the chance to simultaneously admire pictures donated by famous artists and watch the children having their dinner.

Helen thought the practice grotesque but had to concede that it helped raise funds.

'Well, I know the pupils learn music,' said Best, 'but not how to act, surely? Anyway, don't the boys go into the army or navy or get sent off to the Colonies?'

Helen shook her head slowly. 'Many of them do – but some are placed here, as clerks or apprentices. You must recall that scandal when twenty-two boys out of seventy-four who'd been apprenticed to a Yorkshire mill owner died within two years?'

He did. His mind was racing with this new possibility and its implications. He was desperate for more information about Talisman. Their foray into Bloomsbury, calling at his old addresses, had yielded nothing. The man had again managed to retain his anonymity at both places and the visit to the Bodega Bar had been no help either.

They had not found anyone there who knew Talisman but had gained a good impression of the desperation felt by out-of-work actors when they saw them being obsequious to or merely trying to catch the eye of anyone who might give them work.

As she spoke, Helen had been carefully examining Talisman's belongings. She turned over the Hogarth print and was about to replace it on the pile when Best put his hand out to stop her.

'Look at that there. There's writing.' He pointed at some faint pencil marks. 'What does it say?'

Helen squinted at it, then held it up to catch the light from her north-facing studio window.

'Mr G. R. . . . No.' She shook her head. 'I can't quite . . . Just a minute.' She rummaged about in her work-table drawer and pulled out the magnifying glass that she used for fine work. She turned her back so that the light was behind her, held up the print and pushed the glass backwards and forwards to get the words into focus. 'Ah. I've got it!' Slowly she read out, 'Mr G. R. Sims, Lonsdale Square, Barnsbury, Islington. Good heavens!'

They stared at each other and laughed.

'Well, I'm blowed,' exclaimed Best, 'George Sims. Isn't it a small world!'

Lonsdale Square was certainly one of the oddest examples of Barnsbury's hotchpotch of idiosyncratic squares. No Georgian unity of style here.

Built in 1842 when 'London's Dairy', as Islington was called, began its rapid metamorphosis from a place of cattle lairs, pasture land, pleasure grounds and market gardens into a desirable suburb for the Victorian middle classes, the architecture of Lonsdale Square had been described as Elizabethan Gothic but 'ecclesiastical' was the word that had sprung to Best's mind when he had first patrolled through it as a young PC. And that was before he had discovered that these towering, Tudor-gabled houses with their pointed-arch doorways were designed by a church architect.

From the outside, their groups of narrow lancet windows gave the houses a secretive air, but Best had always wondered what they must be like from the inside. Wasn't it odd to have your view of the square's trees and flowers sliced up into long, tall slivers? Had it not been dark, he might have found this out now.

'Ernest! Good to see you!' Sims came forward smiling, his right hand outstretched. As always his ruddy, goatie-bearded plump face was animated.

George Robert Sims had been quite well known to the police and, indeed, the public in general, even before the resounding success of his play, *The Lights o' London*.

Although born into relative wealth and comfort Mr Sims was concerned about the dire plight of many of those who had not been so fortunate. He made it his business to draw attention to it in lectures and his journalism.

He acquired much of his knowledge of the subject from school board officers and the police. Many of them had shown him, as they had Charles Dickens, London's worst slums and most dangerous streets.

Best had been one of these escorts – in the Borough on a Saturday night – and had later been rewarded with tickets for the resulting drama at the Princess's Theatre.

'So disturbed to hear about that poor super, said Sims. He ushered Best into the drawing room and on to a plump Wolsey easy chair, which, with its long soft seat and reclining back, encouraged comfortable relaxation, rather than rigorous interviewing.

Sims held up a whisky decanter.

Best nodded gratefully. 'A small one.'

'Are you going to be able to solve the mystery, d'you think?' he enquired as they sat back companionably.

Best inclined his head and looked rueful. 'I hope so but it's not looking very promising at the moment. Trouble is, I can't find out anything about the man!' he exclaimed with a sudden burst of exasperation. 'It's extraordinary. He worked at a busy theatre among all those people and yet . . .' He stopped, smiled at himself and murmured, 'I thought that maybe you could help.'

'Me?' Sims was taken aback. 'I'd love to of course but I can't see how. I'm not at the theatre that much now the production has been launched. And I can't say I got to know any of the supers.'

Best suddenly realized that this could turn out to be a delicate matter. How stupid of him not to think of that possibility.

He cleared his throat and said casually, 'It's just that we found your name and address on the back of a print among his belongings.'

'Good Lord. How strange.'

Sims put down his whisky glass, sat forward fingering his beard and regarding Best expectantly.

Best related what little he knew about Talisman. None of

it chimed with the playwright until he said, 'Helen thinks he might have been an inmate at the Foundling Hospital.'

'Ah,' said Sims, sitting back. 'That's it, then.'

'You know him?'

''Fraid not. Well, I don't know. But I do have connections with the hospital. I send them theatre tickets from time to time. It's the only time they get out, you know. And I occasionally attend one of their choral concerts.'

Best hesitated but felt he must persist.

'Why should one of the boys have your name and address?'

Sims shook his head, picked up his glass and swirled the amber liquid around. Suddenly, he stopped, put the glass down, held up his right forefinger and waved it about.

'I know. I know what it could be. You know they have their own orchestra?'

Best nodded.

'Well, sometimes they ask me how they can get a job in a theatre orchestra after they come out of the army. You know that quite a number of them get taken on as band boys?'

Best nodded again.

'Well, if they are good musicians, and keen, I sometimes suggest that they contact me when they leave the army and I'll see what I can do.'

'Ah, I see. That's probably it.' Best sat back wearily, trying not to appear too disappointed.

'Sorry, I can't help you more.'

'Oh, that's all right.' Best shrugged. 'At least I now know that Helen is probably right about his being an orphan and I can follow that up.'

'Yes, that's something.'

'We did enjoy the play, by the way – what we managed to see of it! Very realistic. But I must say the Borough has never inspired me like that. I don't know where you get your ideas from.'

Sims laughed as he moulded the right side of his waxed moustache into a finer point. 'Everyone says that. Actually, in this instance, I can tell you *exactly* where I got the idea for the poem which preceded the drama.'

Best and Helen had read his poem 'The Lights of London

Town' before seeing the play. The opening verse, he remembered, had been full of hope:

> The way was long and weary,
> But gallantly they strode,
> A country lad and lassie,
> Along the heavy road.
> The night was dark and stormy,
> But blithe of heart were they,
> For shining in the distance
> The Lights of London lay.
> O gleaming lamps of London
> that gem the city's crown,
> What fortunes lie within you,
> O Lights of London Town!

Needless to say, this hopeful pair had not prospered in the Great Wen. Indeed, quite the opposite to judge by the last verse of several which showed them many years later:

> With faces worn and weary,
> That told of sorrow's load,
> One day a man and woman
> Crept down the country road.
> They sought their native village,
> Heartbroken from the fray,
> Yet shining still behind them
> The Lights of London lay.
> O cruel lamps of London,
> if tears your light could drown,
> Your victim's eyes would weep them,
> O Lights of London Town!

Helen had laughed out loud at its melodrama as she had at Sims's hanky-soaking ballad 'In the Workhouse Christmas Day'. But she appreciated that the man's heart was in the right place. He really was trying to bring attention to the plight of London's poor.

'I got the idea when I was walking back from St Albans.'

62

'Walking back from St Albans!' Best laughed loudly. 'Down on your luck. Or – ' he tapped a finger on his forehead as if pointing to a fount of inspiration – 'was this one of your manic, long-distance walking expeditions?'

Sims chuckled. 'You should be a detective, Ernest.'

'I do try,' said Best. 'God knows, I try.'

Sims had nearly walked Best off his feet in the Borough. He later discovered that the campaigning journalist had become fascinated by the competitive marathon walkers or 'wobblers' who toiled round and round the track at the Agricultural Hall in Islington. As a consequence he had taken up long-distance walking himself.

Only Mr Sims's walking took place out in the open and was not undertaken for the purpose of winning cash prizes but merely for pleasure. He termed himself 'an amateur pedestrian'.

At about 4.30 a.m. he would go to one of the many nearby railway stations, catch a newspaper train to some fairly distant town or village – then walk back.

But St Albans did seem extraordinarily far just for fun. It must be – what – over twenty miles?

It seemed bizarre to Best that what some were induced to do to escape poverty or out of desperation or competitiveness, this comfortably off man was doing for fun.

'I remember exactly the moment,' he said. 'I was just getting near Barnet when I fell in with a young fellow and his wife who were walking to London to find work. They seemed decent folk, so I slackened my pace and walked with them. Night began to fall and, as we came to Highgate, the lights of the City were just visible in the rather misty darkness.'

He smiled at the recollection.

' "Look, Liz," the man exclaimed to his wife as he stretched his hand towards the City, "paved with gold. Yonder are the lights of London." '

Best couldn't quite imagine a working man saying 'yonder' but he supposed that might be what was called artistic licence.

'That night when I got home I had a warm bath as I always do after a long tramp, a light meal and then sat down and wrote the verses.'

Best found it a pleasant change to sit by the blazing fire in this well-appointed room, drinking whisky and chatting. But while endeavouring not to nod off in this reclining chair, the policeman in Best couldn't quite lose the feeling that the motive for all these pleasant revelations about inspiration when walking from St Albans might be to divert his attention from some other matter.

That, in fact, Mr G. R. Sims, the now famous playwright, might know more about Talisman than he wished to admit.

Thirteen

M r Winslet, the Foundling Hospital secretary, was none too happy about 'violating the confidentiality', as he put it, of the Coram Foundation records.

'But the man's dead!' Best protested. 'And we are trying to find out who killed him!'

Consultations with the Master led eventually to what Mr Winslet termed 'a limited opening' of the books. And very comprehensive books they were – in some respects at least.

To Best's surprise, Talisman turned out to be the victim's real name.

'We get so many children here that we run out of names,' said Winslet. 'Some are named after governors and patrons.' He smiled. 'There have been quite a few Corams.'

It had been the shipwright and sea captain Thomas Coram who had founded the orphanage in 1739 after becoming distressed by the sight of so many abandoned babies left dead or dying on the streets of London.

'There were some rather ill-judged flights of fancy,' Winslet admitted. 'Such as naming a child Julius Caesar. But we have reined in that tendency now.'

Best wondered just how a person named Julius Caesar

managed to get through life in nineteenth-century England. Maybe the ignorance of the masses would save him? He knew how he would react if he was dealing with a member of the public who kept telling him his name was Julius Caesar. He might well end up – like the Jesus, King Arthur and Michelangelo he'd come across misbehaving on the streets – in an asylum for the insane.

When a tiny baby Talisman had been handed in to the hospital on 24 November 1856, his real name had been duly exchanged for a number, 20707, and a letter, G. This signified that he was the 20,707th child admitted since the hospital opened in 1740 and the seventh child to be accepted on that particular day. He would later be baptized with a new name.

'Is the mother told his new name?'

Winslet shook his head.

'But what if she wanted to reclaim the child? Surely some do?'

'A few,' Winslet admitted, 'but sometimes even they are refused.'

He sorted about in his file and brought out a small square of stiff paper measuring about eight inches by six.

It was headed: 'Hospital for the Maintenance and Education of Exposed and Deserted Young Children'.

The words, 'exposed and deserted' must have cheered up desperate young mothers, Best thought. He knew that many of them were desperate.

Underneath the date it read: 'Received a . . . . child . . .'

'We fill in whether it is male or female and put in the allotted letter of the alphabet.'

'Their original name is not inserted?'

'No. They will keep their number and letter and that will identify them from then on. But – ' he pointed to the bottom of the receipt – 'this is the most important part.'

> Note: Let this be carefully kept, that it may be produced whenever inquiry is made after the health of a Child (which may be done on Mondays between the Hours of Ten and Four) and also in case the Child should be reclaimed.

'Hand this over and you can get your child back?'

Winslet nodded.

'Was one ever handed in for Talisman?'

'No. I've checked.'

Best thought of his own much wanted child to be. Their admissions procedure appeared rather cold and heartless but he had witnessed some of the alternatives: babies dying from starvation, neglect, and even being murdered.

Best asked for the name of Talisman's mother. He was desperate for more information. The name of Talisman's mother would be something concrete at last but Winslet shook his head.

'No. I'm sorry,' he said and explained, 'I wouldn't have given it to Talisman himself. He would never have known it. So it cannot help you,' he insisted with some justification. 'I *can* tell you that she would have been of good character previous to her "misfortune".'

By misfortune, of course, he meant pregnancy out of wedlock. Children of married women were not admitted unless the fathers had been soldiers or sailors who had been killed in the service of their country.

'A great many of the mothers are domestic servants,' Winslet added in an attempt to sound more helpful.

Best gained a little more information from the Apprenticeship Register.

Winslet did not show this to Best. But by the time the secretary reached the name Talisman among the long list of children sent out into the world in 1869 to learn how to become clerks, pastry cooks, gasfitters, domestics and band boys he had become a little careless.

Best, who had trained himself to read upside-down writing, noticed that bracketed alongside Albert George Talisman as having 'Enlisted in the Band of the 14th Hussars', were two other boys: Kevin Carter and Morris Little.

Winslet didn't offer him this extra information.

'This was among his belongings,' said Best, showing him the locket. 'We wondered if it was one of the tokens the mothers left – or might it be of some other significance?'

Winslet shook his head. We don't accept tokens any more.

The ones you hear about are from the early days. Mothers in the provinces would send their babies in by cart but some of the carters just took their money and didn't bother to deliver the child to us. With tokens if the mothers checked later they would find out if their child had been received.'

'But what did the carters do with the babies?' He thought he knew the answer as he spoke.

'They killed them,' said Winslet.

An astonishing scene greeted Best as he entered the Princess's Theatre auditorium later that morning. There, on the stage, script in hand, was Rosa de la Drake.

A shirt-sleeved Mr Wilson Barrett stood off to her left. Approaching her from the right were Mr George Barrett, the comedian, and Mrs Stephens, the well-known comic actress, the pair who played Mr and Mrs Jarvis, the strolling players in *The Lights o' London*.

'Shakespeare!' Mrs Stephens exclaimed, opening her arms wide in greeting.

'Mother!' Rosa exclaimed.

The pair embraced, Rosa struggling to hang on to her script as they did so.

'Are you quite convalescent, my son and heir?' Mrs Stephens enquired tenderly then, leaning back to take a good look, she added, 'I could eat you!'

'Mother, you—'

'No, no,' interrupted Wilson Barrett. He held up his right hand, palm outwards.

The embracing pair froze in position.

'No,' repeated Wilson Barrett, 'before you say that, Miss Drake, you should laugh in response to your mother's little joke. Then you do a little business, giving each other more hugs and affectionate pats. *Then* you say your next line.'

Rosa nodded, cleared her throat and sent out a little peal of laughter.

'A little deeper, my dear. I know you're a convalescent boy – but you're still a boy.'

Well, why don't you get a boy to play the part, thought Best, not for the first time. This insistence on using women

67

for young male roles puzzled him, although Helen claimed it was often their only opportunity to play a role with any substance.

Rosa laughed a little more deeply.

'Fine, practise that – way down in your throat. Carry on.'

Rosa nodded, laughed a little more deeply, then hugged and kissed Mrs Jarvis exclaiming, 'Mother, you mustn't go without me again!'

'Excellent, my dear, excellent but make sure your kiss is light – don't want your make-up coming off on Mrs Stephens' face, do we?'

It seemed obvious that, for some reason, Rosa de la Drake was taking over the part of the Jarvises' son, Shakespeare, from Esther Gibbons. But, why?

As far as Best could recall, the role of Shakespeare Jarvis was not a huge one. But it was a principal one with quite a number of lines in three scenes: the homecoming at the end of which Mr Jarvis is arrested by the detective Waters, who has mistakenly presumed he is the escaped convict, Harold; Shakespeare and Bess awaiting the arrival of the Jarvises and Harold; and, finally, the scene out on the street where Shakespeare spots the detective again and warns his father.

But why was Rosa reading it? Whatever the reason, it would seem that her rustling petticoat and white kid gloves had repaid the effort and outlay.

'I've been wondering when you'd get around to me!' exclaimed Property Master Alfred Houghton, with a hint of pique in his voice.

'Well,' said Best, 'I realized how important a witness you were. So I wanted to learn more about the business before I got around to you – so I'd know what questions to ask. You see, I'm very ignorant about the theatre.'

It should have been obvious to anyone but an idiot, thought Best, that the real reason was that he had had to concentrate first on the hundreds of 'witnesses' to the murder.

Why, then, did he have to pander to the vanity of people like this twitchy little man with the darting eyes and dry lips that he kept licking? He knew why, to get the best out of them. But it was a tiresome task sometimes.

Helen had warned him that the backstage artisans and professionals – the scene designers and painters, the Property Master and Super Master – felt they didn't receive enough of the credit for the work they did for the fashionable, spectacular productions.

She'd advised him to flatter them, so Best took a deep breath and asked, 'Will you, first of all, describe your work and then tell me exactly how the actors acquire their props.'

'Describe my work! Describe my work!' Houghton exclaimed in a rush like a trained parrot. 'You don't know the half of it. Not the half of it.'

No, but I'm going to find out, thought Best. Why did I give him such an opportunity?

They were sitting alongside a long, heavily stained and battered bench littered with scraps of material and metal foil, lengths of wire, bottles of dye, half-used tins of paint, nails, and every imaginable tool from pliers to hammers, saws to vices.

The air in there was thick with an amalgam of odours: coal gas from the many flaring jets, boiling glue, liquid size and lead paint. Best tried not to breathe in too hard. He could see why the Property Workshop was tucked away at the far end of the theatre's north wing beyond the supers' dressing room and even the lamp room.

'What 'appens,' said Houghton, 'is that when a show is in preparation I'm 'anded my plot. For you that knows nothing about the theatre that is a list of things I 'ave to find and to make for a show.'

As he spoke Houghton was applying glue to two ends of a wooden baton held in a vice but he stopped suddenly to glance up at Best with an almost accusatory glare.

'I have to do it all, you know!' he exclaimed, still holding his glue brush aloft. 'If there's a snowstorm – I 'ave to make the snow an' see it falls right. A fire, and I makes the flames. A train wreck, the explosion an' . . .' he paused for dramatic effect, 'them bodies that are going to be flung about – I make 'em as well. An' it's me what flings them, you know!'

'Good heavens,' said Best, 'I had no idea.'

'People don't! People don't!' Houghton parroted, his eyes blazing. 'They thinks the fairies does it!'

Best looked suitably impressed. 'Amazing.' Truth to tell, he *was* rather impressed. Such a variety of work and skills needed.

To his relief, Houghton put the brush down and applied himself to sticking the two ends together. That done, he caught Best's eye again.

'I makes the spears for the soldiers and the toast an' water mixture that passes for the alcohol to make the hero drunk and I get the guns and load them.'

Ah, at last, the pistol.

'An I 'ave to have another ready to shoot off in the wings in case the first un don't work!'

Two pistols.

'So how,' said Best, 'do the actors acquire their props before a show?'

'They're 'anded 'em,' he said in disgust, ''anded 'em. Don't have to go looking for 'em or nothing like they have to do in the provincials. I ticks them off my list, gives 'em to the call boy and he 'ands them to the actor when he does his rounds.'

'Right.'

'Then the prop is their responsibility. But – ' he held up his right forefinger and wagged it – 'if he has to 'and the particular object to another actor on stage, well then, it becomes *their* responsibility.'

'I see,' said Best.

Fortunately, Houghton had the second imitation pistol which he fired in emergencies and another identical one as a spare. They were both remarkably similar to the real one found lying on the stage after the murder. This had now been identified as an Adams breech-loading .450 as Best had suspected, just like those which had been hurriedly dug out of the Tower of London Armoury to issue to police after the Clerkenwell Explosion but which had ended up in the station safes.

He hoped to God it wasn't one of those. What a scandal that would cause.

Fourteen

It was only at the end of a long day of rehearsals that Best eventually managed to speak to Rosa. He caught up with her as she left by the stage door which led into Castle Street East.

'Why are you reading for Miss Gibbons's part?' he asked bluntly after greeting her.

Rosa couldn't hide her glee.

'She didn't turn up for her performance last night and wasn't to be found at her lodgings this morning,' Rosa explained. 'She'd just upped and left. Couldn't stand it no more, I expect. Some can't all of a sudden. I was making my morning calls when Mr Barrett came looking for a quick replacement. What luck!'

Best frowned.

'But didn't Miss Gibbons have an understudy?'

'Oh, yes. But *she* was understudying several people and they couldn't spare her permanently – so I got the part. I start in two nights!'

'Wonderful!' exclaimed Best, smiling. 'Congratulations!'

She smiled back at him, then looked at him quizzically and asked, 'So, you ... you ... ? Have you been lucky here as well?'

Her exhaustion was making it difficult for her to arrange her thoughts and form her words but she did her best to convey delight at his apparent good luck.

Best was embarrassed.

'No. I have to confess, Miss Drake, that I am not really an actor at all. Just someone wanting to learn as much about the business as possible in a short time – and you helped me with that.'

She looked perplexed. This intelligence seemed more than her rehearsal befuddled brain could cope with at the moment.

They were passing Mrs Sarah Marsh's Refreshment Rooms. Best halted, glanced in and said kindly, 'You must be exhausted. May I treat you to tea and a scone?' He knew that she wouldn't be paid for rehearsals even if she had fares to fork out to get to them.

Rosa nodded gratefully, allowing herself to be steered into the tea shop.

At first, while they waited for their tea and cream scones, Best did all the talking, giving Rosa time to gather herself and relax.

He revealed that he was really a policeman, a detective in fact. This astonished her. He made her smile by describing the amount of acting called for in his job, 'pretending you're not frightened and that you are fully in charge of a situation when in reality you don't know what on earth is going on; pretending to like really nasty people or at least not to be horrified by what they've done – just so you can get them to tell you things . . .' He spread his hands. 'So it goes on . . . Just like you but no one applauds us or calls us back for encores.'

She grinned. 'I will. I think you played a bogus actor very well and deceived a fair maiden to boot.' She clapped her hands in mock salute.

He nodded an acknowledgement.

'Bet you don't get any Latin parts though,' she laughed.

'Ah, but my looks are a good disguise. People expect Scotland Yard detectives to look very British when in fact many of us have at least one foreign-born parent. They need us for our languages to handle all the extradition cases we get these days and for enquiries abroad.'

When their tea and scones arrived she settled down to the business of eating and drinking in a companionable silence.

Her scone finished, Rosa patted her tummy and began to talk. It had been a hard day for her and she was clearly nervous that she might not succeed.

'I do hope I can learn the part in time – I'm so out of prac- tice,' she confided.

'I'm sure they'll make allowances,' said Best. 'It's

important to them as well, you know. They need you and are lucky to have found you so quickly. Remember that.'

He began telling her how interesting he found the theatre world – where nothing was quite what it seemed.

'In what way do you mean?' she asked. Which was what he hoped she'd do.

'Well, for example, I heard that in one play where there was a staged fight some of the supers actually took the opportunity to get in a few digs and punches to one of their own.' He shook his head. 'Extraordinary.'

Rosa nodded thoughtfully.

Best tried again.

'Why do you think that might happen?'

She gave him a sidelong glance, indicating that she realized what he was up to, swallowed her last bite, pushed back her plate, sighed, and said, 'Well, I've only seen that happen once and it was when the fellow was not only a toff but the son of the leading actress. He was hopeless. Had no idea how to move or anything. Absolutely wooden he was. Absolutely wooden. The others were angry because he was taking work from those who needed it.'

'But I thought supers didn't earn enough to make it a full-time job? About a guinea a night, I've been told – and most have daytime jobs elsewhere. They just do it for the fun of it.'

'But not all of them. Some are actors like me who spend the day looking for a proper acting engagement.'

She eyed Best's untouched scone. He pushed it towards her. If bribery was required . . .

She took it, grinned at him and began the cutting and buttering ceremony.

'Besides,' she said when the scone was ready to eat, 'this man, this toff, had been offered a job as a utility – and that made them really angry.'

'Oh, I see,' said Best and sat back to watch her tuck in.

It certainly couldn't be the case here. Talisman might sound like a toff, although in truth he was a poor orphan boy, but there had been no suggestion he'd been offered a utilities' job.

* * *

73

'I think,' said Helen as she wiped her hands and unbuttoned her paint-stained smock, 'that Talisman's mother must have been working at the Princess's. Or he thought she was. Why else would he be so insistent on going there?'

'But how would he *know* she worked there?' Best replied. 'He wouldn't even know who his mother was. The secretary insists that their names are never revealed. The rules state—'

'Now, Ernest,' she smiled at him fondly. Those brown eyes seemed softer since she became pregnant. 'Aren't you the one who always tells me that rules get broken?'

He shrugged. 'True. But they did seem so strict about it – to go to such lengths . . .'

He helped her lower herself into the studio sofa before sitting down beside her. Almost eight months now and she looked fine but a little tired. He wished she didn't work so hard but she wouldn't have married him if she hadn't been able to carry on painting.

'The secretary told me some of the things the mothers do to try to keep in touch with their babies and find out their new names. They plead with him when they come to ask about the health of their child and hang about outside the hospital and get into conversation with the domestic staff.'

Some officers never told their wives about their work but Best could scarcely keep anything from Helen's keen and inquisitive mind. 'You're nosy,' he was always telling her. 'Interested,' she would reply. Truth to tell it was good to share things with her after all the lonely years and sometimes she saw things he didn't. Not that he always liked that.

'Did you show him the locket? Was it a token?'

Best nodded. 'Yes, I did but it didn't signify.' He leaned forward to wipe a smudge of dark blue paint from the side of her face. 'They don't accept tokens any more. Apparently it began in the early days when babies were sent from all over the country and just placed in a basket outside the gate of the hospital. Some of the carriers just took the money for the journey and disposed of their charges on the way.'

Helen went white. 'Disposed of? What do you mean, "disposed of"?'

He hesitated, reached out for her hand and said, 'Killed them.'

She gasped and gripped his hand.

He cursed himself for not remembering that despite her intelligence and education she hadn't been exposed to the harsher side of life. But, then again, she always wanted to know.

'Anyway,' he went on hurriedly, 'when that got out, the governors ruled that every person leaving a baby must leave a token so that they could check whether their child had arrived safely. He showed me some of them: an ace of hearts playing card with a sad verse written on it, several padlocks, old coins, little pieces of embroidery or beadwork. Some had phrases like "Cruel Separation" worked on them.'

'So sad. Poor souls.'

He didn't tell her that some of the little mites were so neglected when they arrived that they died soon afterwards.

'Anyway, they now have a very formal procedure. The applicant has to go for an interview with the governors. If they approve admission, further enquiries are made as to the truth of her claim. If they are satisfactory she is told to bring the baby along on a certain day and is given the receipt in return.' He smiled ruefully. 'It's all very coldly efficient. But at least the children don't starve.'

He could see there was no shame in her. She stood there, her thighs encased in skin-tight pants and the shape of her calves outlined in knee-high leather boots. She was flaunting herself for everyone to see in a way no decent woman should – and striding about like a man! *Pretending she was a young man!*

The anger made his chest tighten so that he could hardly breathe and his nails dug into his palms until they bled as he watched Rosa rehearsing for the scene outside the Jarvises' flat in the Borough.

She was brazen! She was disgusting! He'd tried to put her off. He tugged at his side whiskers until it hurt. He'd told her that it wasn't right. But she wouldn't listen.

Well, she'd learn. By God, she'd learn!

* * *

75

She looks so happy, thought Best, as Rosa entered the refreshment rooms. She also looked decidedly less Spanish. The dramatic deep-pink dress had given way to a demure soft-grey frock topped by a dark-grey cloak. The ruby-red jewellery had been replaced by modest touches of jet.

She moved a little more casually too. There was a little less of the haughty señorita in her carriage and as she sat down opposite Best he was relieved to notice that her perfume was less pungent. When she began to speak, she enunciated a little less carefully but spoke more robustly. A whole new Rosa was emerging.

Shakespeare Jarvis spoke better than his parents, she said but pointed out that he was still Cockney. 'I got to get into the part, ain't I?' she asked with an almost boyish grin. 'Mr Barrett is pleased with me,' she reported, smiling. 'He says I'm one of the quickest learners he's known.'

Learning her lines quickly and performing them had obviously sharpened Rosa's appetite. She fell on the cream scones.

When she finally wiped the crumbs from her full lips and spoke she hadn't much to tell him. The cast was still buzzing about the murder but couldn't help being pleased by the fact that it had made the play even more popular.

Advance bookings were flooding in and that would ensure an even longer run. There wouldn't be any need for those awful nights when a manager looked out at the audience, decided it was too sparse and cancelled the performance – and with it any payment to the actors.

Despite its success, Mr Barrett was already casting for the next production, *The Romany Rye*, another play by G. R. Sims, and Rosa was keeping her fingers crossed.

'If I can get another role there, I'll become part of the company.'

Best thought that this was being a little over-optimistic but he wasn't going to ruin her dreams.

She had learned nothing of interest about Talisman nor how the supers felt about him. Well, he had advised her to be discreet and in any case, as she pointed out, 'I'm one of the principals now and we don't mix much with the supers.'

Mr Barrett's dresser said he seemed to be under something

of a strain, she reported. But that was hardly surprising. It must be a shock to have a murder committed on stage in one of your productions. Particularly if you don't know who did it and what their next move might be.

Of course, if you did it yourself you would have even more reason to be worried. Best hadn't noticed any signs of strain. Rather the reverse. He thought the actor-manager had taken things remarkably well. But his dresser knew him best.

'Some of them laugh and say the reason he is upset is 'cos he hadn't planned the scene beforehand and rehearsed it. Also – ' Rosa giggled – 'he didn't like being upstaged by the murderer. But . . .' she took a sip of tea and leaned forward confidingly, 'his dresser told me on the quiet that he'd been getting some strange letters. Thought he might be being black-mailed again.'

Blackmailed? Again?

Now that *was* interesting.

Fifteen

Arranged around Superintendent Williamson's desk were Best, Smith, Cheadle and Johnson, C Division's local Detective Inspector. Best was endeavouring to put them in the picture regarding the latest developments in what the Press were calling the Death in the Drama Case.

They didn't sound much, he had to admit. Even sorting them out in his own head was proving difficult. The big problem, he reiterated, had been to find out anything about Talisman.

'Until we do that, as you will appreciate, we can't work out why he was killed. At the moment we're following up the boys who joined the 14th Hussars at the same time as Talisman,' he concluded.

'How's that coming along?' asked Williamson.

'Well, good and bad. According to regimental records one of them, Kevin Carter, was discharged for ignominious conduct.'

'Pandering, I expect,' muttered Cheadle.

'No, actually theft,' responded Best. 'Fortunately, they had an address for Carter.'

'I went there,' said Smith, 'but he'd moved on. But we was lucky again. Another lodger knew where he'd gone – so I went there.'

Cheadle sighed heavily and shifted his bulk about in his seat. Always impatient about the how detail, he just wanted to know the results.

Williamson compensated by giving Smith his full attention. He was a kind man. What a pity his kindness had been taken advantage of by the officers involved in the Turf Fraud Scandal of '78. Since then there had been an air of sadness about him.

'But when I got there,' Smith continued, 'Carter was gone again—'

Cheadle sighed with exasperation. 'Do we have to—'

'To Holloway Prison,' said Smith.

Williamson laughed. 'Well, that's good news. We have a captive witness.'

'I'm going to see him there in the morning,' said Best. 'We were less lucky with the other band boy, Morris Little. He left the army when his contract was up and they had no forwarding address for him.'

'I'm surprised he left,' put in Johnson, the local Inspector, anxious to make some sort of impression. 'I've heard they can have quite a good life in the bands – travelling around, being made a lot of—'

'Better outside,' Cheadle announced flatly. With his chin sunk on his chest and his eyes closed he'd been giving the impression he was no longer listening or, more likely, was asleep, again. Apparently not. 'With more music halls starting up all the time there's a big demand for good musicians. They're in competition with the theatre orchestras for 'em but they pay better.' He looked sharply at Best. 'That's where you'll find him, my boy, in a music hall band. What instrument does he play?'

'Several. Trumpet, piano and fiddle.'

'Well, ask around. They all know each other.'

'I will,' said Best.

Williamson steepled his hands and gazed off up to the ceiling. 'I wonder whether we can bring some pressure to bear on the Foundling Hospital to hand over the mother's identity.'

'No point in that,' snapped Cheadle. Then, so as not to appear rude to his superior to whom he was devoted, he softened his manner and went on. 'The foster mother is the one you want.' He thumped the desk. 'What d'you know about her?' he asked Best.

Best was stumped. 'Foster mother? Nothing. I didn't know there was one.'

'Well, they're the ones the children knows an' really cares about. Not the real mothers. No point in tryin' to find them. The children don't remember them.'

The rest of the group looked at each other with raised eyebrows and enquiring frowns, waiting to be educated about foster mothers.

'You don't think they keep all them babies there, d'you?' Cheadle asked, glancing around him wonderingly. 'Course not. They puts 'em out to nurse, don't they?'

The question was a rhetorical one. Not that the wily Chief Inspector would have known what that word meant. He knew lots of other things though.

'If they 'aven't been weaned yet they goes to a wet nurse, and if they 'ave they goes to a dry nurse. The 'ome pays these women well to keep the children till they can walk and talk and are a bit sensible. Anything from three to five years old. Then they bring 'em back and 'and them over.'

Well, how did the old bugger know that? thought Best, not for the first time. And why hadn't Winslet told him about fostering? Maybe thought it was another thing that he didn't need to know. What else had he kept to himself?

Best had always thought that Holloway Prison, built atop a

rise in North London, was the most bizarre example of the mid-Victorian fashion for building workhouses and prisons resembling medieval castles. This huge castellated, red-brick structure was complete with a look-out tower, turrets, battlements, lancet windows and two massive Tudor-style gatehouses.

However, despite its formidable appearance, now accentuated by the fog beginning to creep up its massive encircling wall, the prison did not instil absolute despair in old lags. They knew that, in a regime notorious internationally for its savagery and inhumanity, this mixed-sex prison was regarded as far more humane than most. In any case, it housed only remand prisoners and those on short-term sentences – up to two years. One of these was ex-Foundling Hospital resident, Kevin Carter.

To Best's eye, Kevin Carter was an instantly recognizable type – 'a wrong un' through and through.

He found it hard to pinpoint what it was that signalled a character so negatively to his practised eye. The look wasn't confined to professional criminals, safe-crackers or the like. Nor even persons of known criminality. But Best knew that Carter was a person who, no matter how many helping hands, lenient sentences or last chances he was offered, would always take the crooked path almost as a matter of principle. He would lie even when it was unnecessary; steal at any given opportunity, no matter who was the loser, and strike out violently at the least provocation.

However, such people usually lived by two rules: never help a copper and never tell a copper the truth. He only hoped that in this instance the fate of a fellow orphan might prove an exception to these rules. The only other thing in Best's favour was that the silent system made even the most monosyllabic and solitary prisoners desperate to talk. That, and the alternatives to spending time speaking with him, would be picking oakum and the treadmill.

The warders had told him that Carter was still in the first stage, which meant ten hours hard labour a day with a minimum of six of those spent on the treadmill – a powerful incentive to finding reasons to take time off.

Carter, shaven-headed and prison pallid, sat stony-faced opposite him across a bare table. Best started off by slapping a packet of cigarettes on the table and plunging straight in.

'I need your help,' he said.

A sly and rather incredulous expression began to twitch at Carter's scarred lips.

'It's not for me . . .' Best stopped. No sense in trying to fool a man like this. 'Well, I suppose it is for me in a way. I do want to solve the case. But it's also for the sake of a fellow pupil of yours from the Foundling Hospital.'

Carter's expression did not change. 'Oh, yes?' he said.

He wasn't going to make it easy.

'He's been murdered and I'm trying to find out who killed him and why.'

'Oh, yes?' repeated Carter superciliously but a spark of curiosity now lit his eyes.

Best paused. If I can make him eager to learn more, he thought, gradually provoke him into asking questions, he might soften up a little.

Eventually Carter said peevishly, 'Well, who is it then?'

'He joined the army at the same time as you, same regiment.'

That jolted him a little. 'Not old Morrie Little?'

Best shook his head. 'No, the other one.'

'Oh.' The interest waned. 'You mean young Talisman.'

'I sense a lack of interest,' said Best.

Carter shrugged sullenly.

'I can get you some privileges.'

'Like what?'

'Some extra marks to give you a quicker move on to second stage.'

He sensed that Carter was impressed by that. Second stage meant no hard labour and a mattress five nights out of seven to lay on the plank they slept on. They earned 8 marks a day if they behaved themselves and worked hard and once they had acquired 214 marks they went on to second stage.

But Carter's expression did not change, he just said laconically, 'Oh, right.'

Best sighed. 'Well, never mind . . .' He began gathering up

81

his notebook and prison pass, reached for his hat, glanced at the warder, nodded and made as if to stand up.

'Aren't you going to tell me what 'appened then?!' exclaimed Carter suddenly in a voice so loud that the warder stiffened and reached for his stick.

'If you'll help me.'

Carter sucked his lips. 'I won't rat on no one.'

'I'm not asking you to,' said Best, putting his notebook down. 'Mostly I just want to know what Talisman was like.'

That relaxed him a little. 'Can you get me a visit?'

Best nodded. 'I'll try.' Visits were not allowed until the prisoners had worked their way through to the fourth stage, which, with short-term prisoners, was often never reached.

Best could tell a good tale and he went on to describe Talisman's murder, making it sound as dramatic as possible. It helped that news of the outside world and access to reading matter was only granted in the fourth stage but he deliberately omitted some details so as to force Carter to ask about them. The more Carter talked the more he would loosen up. Sometimes, when such men started there was no stopping them.

'Blimey,' Carter said when Best had finished. 'An' you saw all this?'

'From the stalls,' agreed Best with a rueful grin.

Carter guffawed. 'What a turn-up. An' you can't solve it even though you saw it 'appen!'

'That's right,' said Best, allowing the man his moment of glee.

When he had finished chortling Best put in quietly, 'You don't seem very upset. Didn't you like Talisman?'

Carter shrugged. 'Oh, he was all right. A bit wet. But we was never close. He was in another ward. He an' Little knew each other better. They was in the same ward and Little used to protect him a bit.'

'From what?'

'The older boys, course.' Carter paused, ran his hand over his shaven head and recalled. 'It was worst in the boot room where the lockers were. The masters never went in there. The big boys would run along smacking the smaller ones with a wet towel. That didn't half hurt!' he said indignantly. 'An' they made us fight each other. "Come on fight! Fight you little bastards!" they'd yell, pushing us at each other and giving us a smack if we didn't.'

His face went red and for a moment Best thought he was going to cry. 'Weren't so bad for those who had an elder foster brother to protect them.'

'Did you?'

'No.'

'But Talisman did?'

'Yeah. Well, Little weren't his foster brother or nothing an' he was only a year older than 'im but I think Little – he was big, which was a bit of a laugh – began to feel sorry for the kid.' He paused. 'Might 'ave been something else in it, I dunno.'

'This fostering business,' said Best, 'must be hard on the kids going to the orphanage after being in a real home?'

'They was heartbroken. They didn't know what was going on, did they. Think they belong in a place then suddenly they're just picked up and taken away. Course there was some fosterers that weren't so hot. But even then it was usually better than having nobody. Some foster parents used to be cut-up about it as well.'

'Weren't they allowed to visit the children?'

'The mother could – "the nurse", as they called her. But only once a year. When it came time for us to be apprenticed, some of them tried to get the kid apprenticed to them.'

'I was wondering,' said Best, 'is it possible that an actress might be a foster mother?'

Carter thought for a moment, pursing his lips. Then he shook his head.

'Nah! Can't see that. Most of 'em live out in the country somewhere, Essex or Suffolk or something like that. They have to be respectable as well. They get inspected. Don't think an actress would suit, do you?' He grinned lewdly.

'Perhaps not,' agreed Best, disappointed.

'And you've no idea where Morris Little might be?'

'Nah. He was still serving his time when I left, as you might say.'

Carter reached for the cigarettes and cleared his throat. Best could see the man's mind ticking over. 'Tell you what, I'll have a little think. See if I can come up with anything else. Then you can make another visit.'

'That would be most helpful,' said Best, thinking: It would also get you away from work and you'd receive more cigarettes. He leaned forward. 'Just as a matter of interest, what are you in for? I know it's theft but . . .'

'Van gang,' said Carter, all chipper. 'Down the Commercial Road.'

Van gangs had become something of a menace, particularly on the roads leading from the docks. The robbers made off not only with a van's goods (sugar, currants, tea, tobacco) but with the van and the horse as well. Usually, but not always, they turned the horse and van loose afterwards.

'We was doing well,' he sighed, 'but I took a fancy to this horse – reminded me of one at my foster home in Essex – so I kept it. Wouldn't you know, the owner sees me with it and starts a-hollering. I tries to face it out but – just my luck – the horse recognizes 'im as well and goes over to him! A copper comes along – and there you go.'

Best agreed that life was just not fair. The idea of a tough man like Carter being caught because he took a fancy to a horse was very funny. Touching as well. Perhaps he was wrong about him after all. He must stop making such quick judgements about people.

'Surprised you only got two years.'

'Well – ' he grinned craftily – 'I'm a poor orphan, aren't I? That's what I told the beak – never 'ad a chance. So the old bastard gave me one.'

It was undoubtedly Rosa's night. The last vestiges of the Spanish señorita disappeared as, word perfect, with her hair scraped back and pants more snug than ever, she strode about the stage with all the energy of a young man. The striding was tempered only by the consideration that Shakespeare Jarvis, devoted son of the strolling theatrical family, had recently been laid low with a severe illness.

The sections of the audience who were in the know about this being her first night, or those who knew because they had taken the trouble to read the small slip of paper inserted in their programmes, gave her a specially warm round of applause on entrance.

Only one person, not visible to them, not only withheld approval, but indeed was inflamed the more by the approval of the audience. He swore that he would make her pay for her impertinence.

Sixteen

Best got the impression that Ambrose Harcourt, dresser to Mr Wilson Barrett, was no theatrical hanger-on drawn to the job merely to touch the hem of a star's robe. One who was in the theatre but not of the theatre.

His deep, sonorous voice, which gave every word its proper beginning and ending, and his fluid movements spoke of voice-training and time spent treading the boards. As did his long hair and colourful loose cravat.

'Tell me about Thomas Harris, the dresser who was accused of theft,' asked Best. That, after all, had been the reason given for speaking to this man. That, and the garnering of further information which might help to solve the murder.

Harcourt's mouth tightened at the question. He ceased brushing the coat he was holding.

'For instance, how would he have *become* a dresser at the Princess's?' Best prompted to start him off.

'Well,' said Harcourt eventually as he resumed his brushing. 'It just so happens that I know exactly what he did *before* he came to the Princess's from a letter to *The Era* in which he described his career. His intention was, I believe, to illustrate how varied but how hard theatre life can be but also to show that before his fall he had been trusted by many important theatre managers.'

Harcourt placed the coat back on a rail and looked directly at Best.

'Not unnaturally, being a dresser here myself I took a great interest in what he said. Particularly as his was a life not unlike my own.'

'In what way?'

'Well, like him, I have been engaged in a wide variety of theatre jobs.' He spread his elegant hands in an open gesture. 'For example, like me, he suffered a financial crisis in his life which led him to take a job as a supernumerary – in his case here – under Mr Charles Kean. Then he went on to various other jobs on and off stage until Mr Kean's retirement. After which he was taken on as a dresser to the principals at the St James's, where he was quickly promoted to Super Master. Then he went on tour in the provinces with Mr Charles Dillon as a wardrobe keeper and a general utility actor, playing old men and doing character business.'

Charles Dillon was a popular tragic and melodramatic actor.

'You have a remarkable memory,' said Best.

'As I said, I was interested.'

Harcourt held up his right forefinger to hush Best so he could continue reciting his narrative.

'Then he became the Super Master and Prompter at the Theatre Royal, Rochester, but – ' Harcourt held up both his hands, clapped them together and held them clasped – 'the production was a disaster, an absolute disaster, and he was out of work again and fell ill. He was ill for some time.' Harcourt hesitated. 'I think I have the sequence in the right order.'

Best really was amazed by how well the man remembered all these details about someone else's career. He didn't really need all this information but was loathe to stop him in full flow lest he take offence and cease co-operating.

'Then it was in and out of work again as wardrobe keeper, touring again as super master and prompter – you have to be prepared to take on several roles when on tour,' he added unnecessarily.

'Finally,' said Harcourt, much to Best's relief, 'he became a dresser at Drury Lane, suffered more illness then, in 1877

'...' He drew a deep breath, spread his hands wide and exclaimed dramatically, '... the fatal move. He came here. You know the rest.'

'A varied and busy life,' commented Best.

'Yes, but of course there are always periods without work for most of us and his health did keep letting him down, poor fellow.'

'What is Mr Harris doing now?'

'I've no idea. He sank out of sight.'

After all that! You would think that such interest might prompt more curiosity as to the man's ultimate fate.

'Ask around, will you?'

'Very well. But I don't think he's your man.'

'Really?' Best smiled. 'And why is that?'

'He's a very mild fellow. Not one to harbour grudges, I'd say. And too occupied with husbanding his energy and trying to make a living.' He paused then said vehemently, 'In any case his fall from grace was hardly the fault of this theatre.' He glared at Best, who thought: Oh, it was our fault, was it?

'Wasn't he dishonest?'

'Phish!' exclaimed Harcourt. 'What a silly business that was! Some bits of soap and a few other trifles.'

Best refrained from enquiring whether trifles *were* considered 'the usual dresser's perks', as Thomas Harris's defence had claimed. That might put the man on the spot. In any case, he realized that they probably were.

'Tell me about the duties of a dresser,' he said instead. He was anxious to get to one of the real reasons for this interview – the alleged blackmail of Wilson Barrett. But was wary of being too obvious in case he implicated Rosa.

Harcourt flicked some imaginary fluff from his lapel and looked thoughtful. Best's heart sank. Why had he asked another such open question? It was becoming clear to him that just about everyone backstage felt that they were undervalued and couldn't wait to describe their overwork in great detail.

'Oh, just about everything you could imagine. Everything. I'm a maid of all work – but a happy one,' he added cautiously lest his words should somehow be passed on.

'I look after Mr Barrett's costumes, ensure that his changes are carried out smoothly and that he has any properties he will need on stage. Make him cups of tea and snacks to keep him going and, if necessary, protect him.'

This was more like it.

Harcourt began turning on the mirror lights. As he lit them, their harsh glow showed up his deep cheek creases and stringy neck. It seemed that Ambrose Harcourt was older than he first appeared.

'Protect him from what?' Best asked casually.

'Oh, nothing lethal.' The dresser laughed and paused. 'In an actor-manager's case, like Mr Barrett's, I protect him by seeing that he isn't disturbed by too many unnecessary interruptions on trivial matters which could be dealt with by others.' Harcourt sighed. 'Some actors,' he said with irritation, 'are just like children. They come running to papa over every little thing.'

'We have the same problem with some of our young constables,' smiled Best.

'I also keep out any visitors that I know he would not wish to see – at least until after the performance.'

Best nodded. 'Tell me,' he asked, injecting his voice with the awed air of a Wilson Barrett devotee, 'do you have much problem with members of the public? I mean, Mr Barrett is so famous now . . .'

'Well, they do crowd around the stage door of course. If he's not feeling up to it I endeavour to smuggle him in or out by another entrance but, of course, it isn't wise to do that *too* often.'

'People become offended?'

He nodded. 'And, of course, we have the occasional problem with the blackmailers.'

Best's head shot up.

This was exactly what he had been angling for but he was taken aback when Harcourt broached the subject first.

He managed to tone down his expression to one of general interest before enquiring casually, 'They blackmail actors over their private lives?'

'Oh, no.' Harcourt laughed as, with flowing movements,

he began to pick out certain bottles and jars from a cupboard and set them before the make-up mirror. 'Of course it wouldn't affect someone of Mr Barrett's calibre so much.'

He stopped and looked seriously at Best.

'What they do, some of these loiterers, is offer, quite politely, to applaud the actor during his performance.' Harcourt took a very deep breath as if to gird his loins, then compressed his lips tightly before muttering, 'For a consideration.'

'And if the actor doesn't pay up?'

Harcourt's face reddened and the anger began to spill out. 'They will hiss him down when he is on stage!'

'Good heavens. Why don't you inform the police?'

'Because it happens at all the theatres, and it's bad publicity to make it known. It might even encourage others to take up the practice.'

Harcourt sat down heavily on Wilson Barrett's chair. 'But, believe me, less than half a dozen men acting in concert can make such a disturbance as to render it wholly impossible for an actor to continue!'

It was obvious by the vehemence and hurt in his voice that he himself had been a victim of such cruel treatment.

Helen was aghast at the very idea of the blackmailers casually destroying an actor's career although she herself had often had her work dismissed as trivial and worthless just because she was a woman.

When Best pointed this out, she said, 'Oh, yes but we professional women are used to being undermined, my dearest.' She spooned him out a substantial portion of rabbit pudding. 'We expect it even. So we are not so devastated when it does occur.'

He wasn't sure that was true. He'd seen her very hurt by such dismissals.

She handed him his plate. The pudding smelled rich and herby and quite delicious.

There was no doubt that his meals had improved since his marriage. Not through Helen's efforts but those of their cook, Jessie, the young girl Helen had taken in after Best had rescued her from a father who beat her and made her pregnant.

That was three years ago now and although devoted to Helen her enthusiasm and repertoire of dishes had expanded rapidly now that she had a man to please as well.

Best helped himself to mashed potato, buttered parsnips and boiled cabbage.

'In fact,' she said, returning to the subject, we women painters are criticized whatever we do. If we paint babies and domestic scenes, that just shows how limited our lives are – and our vision. If we paint the world outside we are tackling something quite beyond our experience and being unfeminine at the same time.'

Best nodded and tucked in. He was about to point out the amazing welcome received by Elizabeth Thompson's *The Roll Call,* which showed a bedraggled line of weary British soldiers huddled in greatcoats against a snowy landscape. But he thought better of it. He'd found that it was better to say nothing at these moments. They rarely lasted long.

'And look at those actresses in breeches roles. One minute critics are saying how wonderful they are and the next criticizing them for overstepping the mark with their costumes and revealing just a little too much.' Helen speared a piece of pudding. 'Showing that women have legs. How dreadful! Do you know, some serious actresses are so worried about their reputations that they are refusing to play Rosalind or Viola? The joke is that when Shakespeare wrote those parts it was men playing women! It's all too ridiculous.'

Best gathered the last of his potato into a dam for the delicious meat and gravy.

'Must have seemed even stranger then,' he agreed. 'Think of it. A man playing a woman disguised as a man who then revealed she was a woman but in reality was a man!'

Helen stopped eating, looked at him, raised her eyes to heaven with an expression that revealed that she knew exactly what he was doing. Then she giggled and said, 'Love to have seen it.'

'Me, too.' He could always make her laugh.

She pointed to the rabbit pudding and lifted her eyebrows.

Best nodded. 'A little, please.' He held out his plate.

'So,' she said as she refilled his plate, 'did you broach the subject of blackmail letters?'

He sighed dramatically. 'I certainly don't need Cheadle to check up on me when I've got you,' he teased, then admitted, 'Well, it was difficult. I didn't want him to suspect that Rosa had been breaking confidences. Eventually I edged into the subject by a side wind.'

Helen laughed. 'How did you do that?!'

'Oh, nothing clever. Later on, after we'd talked about the stage-door blackmail, I asked if the principals ever received blackmail letters about their private lives. He just shook his head and said he didn't know as it wasn't one of his duties to open other people's correspondence. I felt very coarse and vulgar for asking such a question.'

'Well, you are my dear, you are.' His wife smiled fondly. 'It's one of the things I love about you.'

He smiled wanly. 'I only hope I haven't put Rosa in any danger by asking. He didn't seem too happy.'

She rang the bell.

Jessie must have been outside the door as she came in almost instantly. It was one of her regrets that they insisted on serving themselves.

'Delicious, Jessie,' said Best. 'You're a marvel.'

She grinned with pleasure. 'Ta, Mr Best.'

'What's for pudding?'

'Apple amber.'

'Oh, heaven. My favourite.'

'They're all your favourites, sir.' She giggled cheekily.

'I suppose they are,' he admitted. 'How clever of you to notice that.'

'Ernest Best, you're incorrigible,' Helen exclaimed when she'd gone, ' – even charming the cook.'

'Who better, too?'

'No one,' she admitted. Then, returning to their discussion, she asked, 'Now, why should Rosa be in any danger? Harcourt's not your killer, is he?'

'Who knows? He could be.'

She shook her head. 'I don't think he did it.'

'Someone else who knows best. Harcourt informed me it

couldn't possibly be Thomas seeking revenge because the man was too mild and distracted by earning a living.'

'Well, there you are then.'

'There I am, what?'

'If Harcourt was the killer he wouldn't be putting you off another possible suspect, would he? He'd be encouraging you to add him to your list.'

Seventeen

It was late. Most of the cast had left their dressing rooms. Some had gone to the stalls bar, which, as the notice on the dressing-room walls advised, was kept open for half an hour after the end of the performance 'for the convenience of the artistes'. Others had gone home.

In the two ladies' dressing rooms in the east wing of the dress-circle floor, only Rosa and Mrs Stephens, who played Mrs Jarvis, remained.

Rosa had been delayed by the wardrobe keeper, who had been anxious to make an adjustment to the new principal's costume. Well, more than an adjustment, a repair. Rosa's well-rounded hips had strained the stitching at the back of her breeches, putting her in danger of revealing even more of her seductive shape than had originally been intended. Now there was this note from Mr Barrett saying he wanted to see her in half an hour's time.

Mrs Stephens picked up her handbag and adjusted one of her old-fashioned bonnets without which she was never seen offstage.

'Aren't you coming, dear?' she asked.

Rosa shook her head. 'Mr Barrett left me a note asking me to meet him in the Painting Room.'

Mrs Stephens frowned. The Painting Room was a lofty

space way back stage behind the flies on the upper circle where scenery for the next show was produced.

'I expect he wants to go over that business where you say about seeing the detective.'

Rosa was all too aware that that line of hers had gone wrong tonight. She was very anxious about it.

She had said the words, 'There's the tec,' before the actor playing Waters the policeman had got into position. She knew the audience must have been puzzled.

'Don't worry about it, my dear.' Mrs Stephens patted her shoulder. 'We all make little mistakes like that – even when we have been playing the part for months.' She paused. 'Strange place for him to want to see you at this time of night though. Are you sure you've got it right?'

'That's what I thought,' Rosa agreed nervously.

She wasn't looking forward to finding her way up there to those deserted backrooms in the semi-darkness, particularly as she still had trouble finding her way around.

'Oh, *I* know,' exclaimed Mrs Stephens. 'I expect he'll be looking over *The Romany Rye* scenery – I hear there's going to be a shipwreck! He'll be seeing how they're getting on with it while nobody's about. The man never rests!'

The Romany Rye! Rosa was hoping that her dark good looks might help win her a role in that forthcoming production. She'd heard that the play was going to be amazing. Fantastic sets, with everything from a gypsy encampment to a shipwreck and a cast of about forty. Of course Wilson Barrett was to play the hero, Jack Hearn the gentleman gypsy. His brother and Mr Willard would be given other male leads but, she'd heard, there weren't many big parts for women.

Obviously, Miss Eastlake would play the starring role of Gertie, the daughter at the big house, with whom Jack falls in love. But Rosa had her eyes on the part of her rival, Kiomi Lee, a warm-hearted gypsy girl.

Rosa stared at herself in the mirror. Should she insinuate a hint of the gypsy into her appearance? Let her hair become a little wild, tumble her curls about her face? She'd have to be careful not to look old fashioned or wanton. Maybe some time when she'd let down her hair before scraping it back and tying it up to play Shakespeare she could find a reason to bump into Mr Barrett and—

'Goodnight, my dear,' said Mrs Stephens, breaking into Rosa's reverie.

The young woman glanced up absently. 'Good night, Mrs Stephens. Hope you have a good journey home.'

'So do I,' she replied, 'so do I. One of the horses went lame last night and I'm sure the other one was blown. It looked pleased at getting some rest anyway.' She laughed. 'But poor me had to wait an age until another omnibus came along.'

After she had gone, Rosa looked up at the dressing-room clock – always kept strictly accurate – still ten minutes to go before she was due at the Painting Room.

She busied herself tidying her make-up pots, making sure they did not overlap Emmeline Ormsby's space. Emmeline played Hetty Preene – an awful part. Even *The Theatre* had commented on what an unsympathetic role it was. They had pointed out that Hetty was an unredeemably bad and heartless woman, adding cruelly, 'to which Miss Ormby's acting style is scarcely suited'.

And here am I coming in as the popular Shakespeare Jarvis and getting all this attention. Emmeline must find that irritating.

Rosa was aware that it was vital for her to keep in with her fellow players if she wanted to become part of this company. And she did. Oh, how she did.

Could this meeting amongst the scenery for *The Romany Rye* be a good sign? she wondered. Maybe Mr Barrett wanted to show her her caravan or one of the other scenes in which she would play?

Rosa pulled herself up. She was being fanciful. She had had too many disappointments in this business to allow her imagination to carry her aloft for too long. Now and again she allowed herself a fantasy treat on the understanding that she remembered that was what it was – a lovely dream. Always there was that little voice in the background reminding her not to let her hopes climb too high. Things were bound to go wrong again and she'd have further to fall.

Time to go.

Suddenly, she leaned forwards towards the mirror, snatched out the pins, which held her hair back into a chignon of curls, then shook her head hard to free them until they tumbled around her cheeks and cascaded on to her shoulders.

She reached over to Mrs Stephens's costume rail, scooped up the black woollen shawl the older woman wore to go shopping in the Borough Market and flung it carelessly around her shoulders. 'There you are,' she told herself firmly. 'A gypsy woman to the life.'

She turned off the gaslights around her mirror. How quiet it was back here now.

The silence was eerie in a place usually so full of chatter while outside there would be the clatter of actors dashing back and forth along the corridor, the distant sounds of the audience, and the music from the stage.

She must be the only person left on this floor. The natural creaks and groans of a cooling building, scarcely heard normally, now sounded like cracks of thunder and made her jump with fright.

She took a deep breath, patted at her curls, drew herself up into a dignified yet earthy pose, opened the door and went out into the silent corridor.

Eighteen

'The fire?' asked Alfred Houghton, the Property Master. 'Oh, that scene in *The Streets o' London*? One of the best scenes ever. Nobody had seen anything like it before. It were the talk of London, I'll tell you. The talk of London.'

'No, actually I was thinking of the real fire – the one with those poor dancers. Someone was telling me that—'

'An' told you all wrong, I'll warrant,' broke in Houghton. 'I was there, an' I saw it! It was terrible. Terrible! Those poor girls! Those poor girls! I can still see them now – an' smell their charred flesh.'

'What happened?'

Best hoped he would be spared too much detail about the charred flesh.

He was sitting in Houghton's workroom again, breathing in the odours of rabbit glue, turpentine and the dozen other unpleasant substances which blended into a potent mixture, while the twitchy Property Master fashioned a primitive weapon for possible use in *The Romany Rye*.

'You gotta get started early with these things,' he'd insisted, 'get ahead of the deluge. This script has three attempted murders, a burglary with violence and two abductions. That's a lot of work for me – a lot of work.'

Smith was out trying to track down Morris Little, the third band boy. Best, uncertain what to do next, had settled on 'just chatting' to various backstage workers. In his experience, the more people saw you about and the longer you chatted about matters inconsequential, the more they would forget you were a policeman. Then important information might slip out unnoticed.

'It was pantomime, of course, pantomime. And it was the dancers of course, the dancers. It was always them.'

'Why's that?' asked Best although he knew why.

'Them dresses the ballerinas wear. Them flimsy dresses with all them layers of petticoats.' His glance darted to Best, then back to the weapon. 'Lovely they look. Like real women should.'

He pulled a piece of metal from under the bench and began hammering and shaping it into a curve. This was going to be a protracted business and Best wondered whether he really should be elsewhere, doing something else. But what?

'Course, the trouble was they had to dance right by them footlights. Them gas jets didn't have no guards or nothing then – all you needed was a little draught – and away!' He flung his right hand wide.

Best shook his head. 'Terrible. Terrible. So one of the ballet girls was dancing near the footlights and—'

'Oh, no,' said Houghton. 'That weren't it *that* time. It were

96

a spark from one of the coloured light batons in the wings. The dress of this girl, Ann Hunt she was called, caught on fire. Her friend, Sarah Pearman, tried to put out the flames but caught fire herself. They ran across the stage to the other ballerinas but they backed away from them – frightened they'd catch fire as well. Not surprising. The audience was screaming. They'd seen the girls all alight. In the end, it were the stage manager what put the flames out – an got badly burned himself.' Houghton put down his hammer and perused his work. 'Wouldn't have happened like that if Mr Kean had still been in charge,' he announced firmly. 'No, it wouldn't have happened if 'ed been there.'

He began hammering again, waiting for Best to ask, 'Why not?'

The Detective Inspector obliged.

'Because,' answered Houghton, holding up his piece of metal and examining it again, 'Mr Kean always insisted that there were wet blankets and water pots by the stage and that there was somebody there to use them – under pain of a big fine if they was absent.'

'And the girls? Didn't one of them die?'

'Yes. That Sarah Pearman. She had terrible burns. Terrible. She was only seventeen an' would never have got burned if she hadn't tried to help her friend.'

Best shook his head. 'And the other girl?'

'She had terrible burns as well, all down here.' He drew his hands down from his chin, over his chest and arms.

'So, what happened to her?'

'Well, she lived, but of course couldn't dance no more.'

'Where did she go?'

'I dunno. Back home to her mam and dad I suppose.' He paused. 'And do you know what? The very next Christmas – *the very next Christmas* – in *another* pantomime in *another* ballet scene – *another* dancer's dress caught fire!'

'Was that at the Princess's as well?'

Best had vague recollections of this but there were so many women whose dresses caught fire both on the stage and in their own homes that their sorry tales tended to merge in his mind.

97

'No. That was at *The Pavilion*. But it was just the same story. The same story.'

'Did she die?'

He nodded. 'A couple of weeks later.'

So, the Princess's wasn't the only theatre in which people had reason to hate a neglectful management.

But the Princess's fire had happened back in the sixties. Would hatred have festered that long? And would it cause someone to kill another member of the cast?

Best realized he was attempting to apply rationality to something which was often irrational. Of course hatred could fester that long and burst out suddenly many years later. But when that happened, usually there was something that brought it out again. What could it be in this case? The success of the current play?

The popularity of *The Lights o' London* that was filling the house every night and earning plaudits and a great deal of money for the writer and management?

Maybe the killer was demonstrating that none of this happens without the badly paid, hard-working smaller fry – such as the poor burned dancers? Those who, like so many resentful members of the backstage staff, felt they didn't receive due attention or reward and whose safety was given scant attention. First in fire prevention and now in care over firearms?

Then again, the fire had occurred several managements back – during the seven-year reign of ex-bank clerk, actor-manager George Vining.

Maybe the murderer was unconcerned about which management it was? Maybe didn't even realize it had changed? To him it was the Princess's and that was all that mattered.

And, maybe I'm barking up the wrong tree, thought Best.

As he watched Houghton hammering and painting, his mind began to drift away and the nervy little man's voice with its rushed delivery and repeated phrases sank into the background.

There is some connection here that I'm missing, he reflected. Some link, some pattern that is evading me.

I'm tired, he admitted. I'm just not able to go on and on

like I used to. But, dammit, I should be able to. I'm only thirty-six. Maybe it's because I now have something to stop for, someone to go home to. Another life which I don't want to miss.

What I need to do, he persuaded himself, is to slacken off a little. Then this connection will just pop into my mind. It had happened before.

Was this just an excuse to remove himself from the smells and the noise of this workshop and the artificiality of the theatre scene and get back home to the reality of Helen and their unborn child?

What if it was? he decided suddenly. I don't care!

He left the workroom and its noxious smells, walked out of the theatre into a still daylight Oxford Street, stopped by a flower stall, bought a large bunch of yellow asters and gold chrysanthemums, and went home.

Nineteen

Mrs Stephens was applying her make-up in front of her dressing-room mirror. Many years' practice using greasepaint to transform herself into variations on the jolly, comic, middle-aged woman had made her movements swift and deft. As she grew older, less artifice was required. Some wrinkles were already present, so the whole procedure became even less demanding.

The result of these roles was that she spent a great deal of time in the company of much younger women who played her daughters or granddaughters or, as in this case, her son.

Sometimes she found their trivial prattle irritating but mostly she didn't mind. Their optimism cheered her.

It was now twenty minutes to opening time and the chatter of Emmeline and Lizzie had abated while they concentrated upon hiding their actors' pallor and transforming themselves into the pretty but heartless Hettie and the down-and-out Sal.

The only one missing was Rosa, which was most unusual.

Rosa was usually the first to arrive. When the other girls rushed in after a little last-minute shopping at Peter Robinson's or looking a little pink-cheeked from a quick canoodle with a gentleman friend near the stage door Rosa would be there diligently reading through her lines. But not tonight.

There was a sharp rat-tat-tat on the door. Wilson Barrett making his usual pre-performance rounds.

'Everyone here? Everything all right?' he shouted.

Mrs Stephens hesitated. She didn't want to get the young actress into trouble. Rosa was so keen to do well and to impress Mr Barrett and she was bound to come dashing up the stairs any minute.

'Yes, fine,' she replied but the unease had crept into her voice.

'Are you sure?' asked Mr Barrett, opening the door slightly.

'Well,' Mrs Stephens admitted, 'Rosa's not here yet, which is most unusual,' she added hastily. 'I'm sure she'll arrive any minute . . .'

Mr Barrett looked annoyed. 'Well, if she's not here in five minutes, Lizzie had better begin making up as Shakespeare. Annie can double as Sal. And *you* come and tell me.' There was a note of censure in his voice. 'Then go through Shakespeare's lines with Lizzie.'

Rosa had still not appeared by the time Barrett, in a shabby suit and soft hat, his costume for Harold, the destitute prodigal son returning to beg his father's forgiveness, emerged from his dressing room on the ground floor near the stage.

Mrs Stephens could see that he was furious.

In the theatre, reliability was as important as acting talent. What was the point in being able to wring hearts or strike terror into them with your performance, if you couldn't be relied on to turn up to do it? Not only that, unreliable actors caused fellow artistes much anxiety and inconvenience.

Rosa had better have a very good explanation, thought Mrs

Stephens. If not, a large fine would be levied on her and no further engagements be forthcoming.

Although her own entrance was not for some time Mrs Stephens had thought it politic to be down by the stage alongside Barrett and the pale and equally shabbily dressed Mary Eastlake.

'Was she all right last night?' Barrett asked, his voice tight. 'Not ill or anything?'

Mrs Stephens shook her head. 'No. She seemed fine. Fine.'

Wilson Barrett was strict with his rules and firm about extracting fines if they were disobeyed but he did care about the health of his employees. Unlike some.

'As a matter of fact she was still here when I went home. Rosa was the last one left in the dressing room. She was waiting to come down for her meeting with you.'

Barrett stared at her. 'Meeting? What meeting?'

'Well, she didn't know what it was for. She thought it might be about that slip she made in the Borough scene – her saying "There's the tec" before he'd arrived.'

Barrett waved his right hand back and forth dismissively. 'Oh, that was nothing. Nothing! We all make little mistakes and she's done remarkably well – until now.'

'Well, why *did* you want to see her?'

'I didn't!'

'Oh. But she told me that you had sent her a note saying to meet you in the Painting Room half an hour after the performance.'

'What?' He looked at her with disbelief. 'What note?'

He was clearly very angry. She could tell by his clipped tones. He must think Rosa had made it up.

'She was telling people I'd sent her a note for a clandestine meeting in the Painting Room after the performance!' he exclaimed incredulously. 'This is ridiculous!'

Oh, dear. Rosa was done for now. The actor-manager hated 'mischief-makers' in his company. And it must seem to him that that was exactly what Rosa was.

The police station furniture from the last act usually slid smoothly back into place in the scene dock which was situated by the side of the stage.

Tonight, it didn't.

Tonight, it stuck.

The scene-shifters were impatient, having at last reached the end of their long and busy evening's work, which began just after 6 p.m. First, they prepared the stage for *A Photographic Fright,* the farce that preceded the main production. Then, from 7.45 p.m. on, they coped with no fewer than ten complicated changes of scene for *The Lights o' London* which had to be executed with great speed and precision.

Despite a programme note requesting the audience's indulgence during 'the elaborate scene changes' they did sometimes show their impatience when kept waiting. Particularly the more unruly elements in the pit. So, the scene-shifters' work was heavy and stressful and by the last scene they were exhausted.

It was 11 p.m. and newcomer Joe Burridge and old hand Harry Edgar had had enough. There had only been the final tidying away to do before they could have a pint and go home. Now this blessed thing had stuck.

'Here, help me give it another push, Harry,' said Joe, straining against the upright batons. 'It came out easy enough. It should go back in the same way.'

It didn't.

'Hold on,' said Harry, 'I expect some idiot actor has left some props in the way.'

Idiot actors were the bane of the lives of stagehands.

Harry went into the scene dock interior to investigate. Joe waited patiently.

There was a few moments' silence, then a high-pitched muttering, 'What's this? What's this?' followed by horrified shouting, 'Oh, my God! Oh, my God!'

Harry came rushing out, ashen-faced and yelling, 'Get the boss! Get the boss!'

'What *is* it?' asked Joe, perplexed.

'Get the boss! Get the boss!' was all he could get from the grey-faced Harry, who was propping himself up against the scene dock wall.

Joe began to move then stopped in confusion. 'Which one?' he asked. 'The foreman or Mr Barrett?'

'Mr Barrett! Mr Barrett!' exclaimed Harry.

Must be something terrible. Had someone been damaging the scenery?

'No need to shout. I'm here,' said Wilson Barrett, approaching from the stage, 'and,' he added sharply, 'I hope you have a good excuse for making all this noise. The play may be over but many of the audience are still in the building.'

Joe pointed to Harry but Harry was unable to speak, indeed seemed about to be sick. He pointed towards the interior of the scene dock, then managed to whisper, 'It's in there.'

Twenty

The body was curled over into a foetal position. From what they could see there were no obvious signs of injury. But then the front of her body was obscured and her tumbling curls and the man's cap on her head might hide any wounds on her head.

They didn't want to examine it further until the police surgeon got there but one thing was certain. She was dead. Quite dead and decomposing.

Harry, who after retching in a corner for a while had recovered his power of speech, was now unstoppable. He was quite certain of the cause of her death: a backstage accident or fall.

Actors, as he pointed out, were always being warned about the dangers backstage. It was true, the risks were legion, particularly in the flies, which had sufficient ropes to equip a medieval man-o'-war. Then there were the pulleys, drums, windlasses, counterweights, traps, sliders and gas battens. Add to these careless carpenters who dropped hammers from on high and gas hazards and . . .

Even the scene dock had its risks with sharp edges to catch

yourself upon, lumps and bumps to trip over and scenery which could topple at any moment.

'They're always being told,' said Harry, endeavouring to re-establish his status as the imperturbable old hand who was surprised by nothing. 'But will they listen? No.'

Of course they all realized that it probably was not an accident. But at present no one wanted to contemplate that possibility. Clearly, if it was an accident it was odd that her body had remained undiscovered during the evening's production activity. Not to mention that of the previous evenings since she had gone missing.

Partly for these reasons Best did not doubt for a moment that it was murder. She had clearly not died there tonight but her body had been placed there then.

When he eventually left the theatre in the early hours, he was thinking, I have never had such a strange case. Or was it two separate cases? Whatever it was, the effect on the company had been devastating. No convivial backstage chat any more or trips to unwind at local hostelries. A pall of fear and depression had settled over them.

Were the murders linked in some way or did they have nothing whatsoever to do with each other? Surely that was unlikely? Two murders in one theatre in a matter of a few days. The odds against that must be astronomical.

But if they *were* linked – how? What could possibly be the connection between the dramatic onstage murder of Talisman, a lonely orphan super, and the death of one of the principal actresses?

They would know better when the post-mortem revealed whether Miss Esther Gibbons, whose disappearance had given Rosa her big chance, had been raped or sexually assaulted before her death. Also, how long she had been dead and what had been the manner of her demise.

All Best had been able to establish before the body had been removed was that her face had a blueish tinge, there was no longer any rigor mortis, in her hand was a button and a piece of grey material, possibly torn from the garment of her attacker and, grotesquely, a cigar had been stuck in her mouth.

There was no doubt about the dissimilarity of the actual

crimes even lacking that diagnosis. Talisman had died violently in the most public way possible, on stage before an audience of three thousand, while Miss Gibbons had been killed stealthily.

That was unusual. Murderers tended to have a favoured method.

One thing the killings did have in common. There was no apparent motive for either.

If they were connected, it really did appear that the perpetrator must be someone with a grudge against the theatre and who was unhinged enough not to baulk at murdering two innocent people in furtherance of their quest for revenge.

Revenge for what? Best could only think of the burning of the ballerinas in the fire – even though that happened almost too long ago to be feasible. Then again, there was the dresser who had been caught stealing.

Then yet again, he sighed, there were doubtless dozens of other resentments bubbling away beneath the surface. The theatre was a closed world and animosity over real or imagined injustices must build up even in the best run of them.

Best halted suddenly outside the London Crystal Palace Bazaar by Regent's Circus North as a thought struck him.

He'd forgotten about the possibility of a threat from a rival theatrical company.

Barrett had dismissed the idea, saying that they needed each other's success. Best had just accepted that, but now he wondered whether that was strictly true. Surely a great success, like *The Lights o' London*, would draw potential audiences away from its rivals?

Well, there was only one that provided equally dazzling melodrama and that, as Barrett had admitted, was the Lyceum under the actor-management of Henry Irving. He shook his head in disbelief at his own thoughts – that was an outlandish idea. There must be simpler ways of sabotaging a rival? In any case Henry Irving had also declared that theatres needed the success of others as this encouraged audiences to adopt the theatre-going habit.

There were the music halls, of course. Two of them in Oxford Street alone. But, if anything, it was they who were winning working-class audiences away from the theatre whilst the middle and upper classes were now finding the theatre more acceptable because it was more respectable. So, wasn't there a mutual need?

Besides, the first murder had increased bookings at the Princess's, not diminished them. So the revenge idea fell down there.

Of course, a second murder might be a murder too far – even for a bloodthirsty public. Come to that, the Lord Chamberlain could start enquiring about the running of a theatre which allowed such things to occur.

Best shifted his focus to think around the subject as he was always instructing Smith to do but sometimes forgot to do himself.

What about those people who were enraged by the realistic depiction of the sleazier side of London life? As in *The Lights o' London,* which showed thieves and prostitutes in the Borough at midnight, and the prison brutalities in *It's Never to Late to Mend.* But surely this would not make anyone angry enough to commit murder?

You're doing it again, he thought. Applying rationality to what was often an irrational act. You know it doesn't work like that.

But, before he followed up any of these possible links or ideas he must make the sensible initial actions in any murder inquiry. That is, learn more about the victim, the late Miss Gibbons. With luck, as well as a motive for murder this might reveal a link between her and Talisman.

Could *she* have been the reason he wanted to work at the Princess's? Might she even be the lost foster sister? Carter had described how they were cruelly separated when brought back to the Foundling Hospital after being fostered.

He would ask around the theatre. Talk to more people. Find out what kind of girl Miss Gibbons had been. While he was doing this he would probe for hints of enemies of the theatre and its management. For example, just why was Wilson Barrett being blackmailed?

In the meantime, he would send Smith off to enquire at Miss Gibbons's home address.

It would be good experience for him. So far John George had been unable to find Morris Little, the third Foundling Home orphan of the trio which had become army band boys. Best was very keen to find this man. The gun used to kill Talisman had been an army issue and at one time Little had been a soldier. He had a nagging feeling Morris Little held the key to the Talisman mystery. Or was he just clutching at straws?

He pushed to the back of his mind the fact that over six hundred such army weapons had been issued to the Metropolitan Police. That was one complication too many for him to contemplate just now.

Maybe Littlechild would trace up the third bandsman for him? That would be right up his street. He spoke theatre language and had lots of stage connections through his membership of the Metropolitan Police Minstrels.

But the thought that haunted Best most of all, as he gave up walking and hailed a cab, was the possibility that the murders were *not* linked after all and that they had a sex murderer on their hands. One who might strike again.

He had told Mr Barrett to warn all the women. But he knew that after the audience went home a theatre was a rambling place with many empty rooms, dark recesses and deserted corridors.

Ideal places in which to lie in wait.

Twenty-One

'This note I was supposed to have sent you – ' said Wilson Barrett crisply.

'Supposed!' exclaimed Rosa. She was mortified. He thought she'd made it up! 'I did receive a note,' she exclaimed. 'I did!'

'*How* did you receive this note?'

'It was on my dressing table when I arrived.'

'I don't suppose you have still got it?' His voice was even but icy cold.

She realized that her agitation and the blush rushing up her neck must make her appear guilty of his unspoken accusation. Her nightmares were coming true. She was going to lose her part and be back to begging agents for work.

It had been bad enough trying to explain why she had failed to appear on time for a performance. That she had been to see her sister Betty.

Betty lived in Silvertown, a strange and desolate Thameside area not long since a marsh and now the site of a shipyard and a variety of chemical and engineering factories with workers' houses in between.

Betty's husband Jack was employed at Henley's Electric Telegraph Works. She was stuck at home with three children under five and with only factory walls to greet her when she went out. She couldn't wait for Rosa to come and tell her about her success as an actress at the famous Princess's Theatre.

Betty had been a seamstress and found time even now to make some of Rosa's clothes which was another reason Rosa had gone to see her. Given her new status, she felt even more need to maintain a good appearance and she needed a new winter coat.

Not that Rosa explained all this to Mr Barrett but she did tell him how she'd gone by train, on the North London Line, to make sure she'd get back in plenty of time. Also, that on the return journey there had been a breakdown and everything had come to a halt and how she had tried desperately to get back for the performance.

Mr Barrett commented that she should make sure she allowed sufficient time for such emergencies or not go at all. Then he had lectured about her new responsibilities. She explained that she had allowed three hours and he'd replied that obviously that was insufficient.

Rosa had accepted this chastisement even though she knew that if she had earned as much money as Mr Barrett she would have been able to get a cab back instead of ride on omnibuses which took for ever.

In the end, he'd said not to let it happen again, told her she would have to pay a fine and that there was another matter he wished to discuss with her, later.

His manner had been severe and she wondered what on earth the other matter could be. Now she knew. It was the letter. He thought she had made it all up! Why hadn't she kept it?!

She shook her head and admitted wretchedly, 'I threw it away.'

'I see.'

No you don't! No you don't! Rosa shouted inwardly.

All her reawakened dreams were falling to dust. He had seemed so pleased with the way she learned her lines and what he called her rapid grasp of the nuances of the part . . .

Now his glance was contemptuous.

'What did this note say?'

'It said . . .' Rosa thought back. She had to get it right and try not to gabble. 'It said, "Dear Miss de la Drake, There is a matter I wish to discuss with you. Please meet me at 11.30 p.m. in the Painting Room." '

Barrett held her eye. 'And it didn't occur to you that there was something strange about that?'

'Yes, it did. It did!' she insisted. 'But I'm new here and I haven't yet learned all your habits and practices,' she rushed on, then took a deep breath in order to regain control. She mustn't lose control. 'Mrs Stephens was puzzled as well, at first.' She knew that Mr Barrett valued Mrs Stephens's opinion. They were old colleagues from years back. 'But then she told me that perhaps you were having a look at *The Romany Rye* backcloths, seeing how they were coming along.'

He inclined his head in acceptance of this as a possibility.

'So, what happened when you got to the Painting Room?'

'Nothing.' Rosa was trying desperately to hold back her tears. 'It was dark and I couldn't find it. I don't know my way around backstage yet – I haven't had the time . . .'

He said nothing.

'So I went downstairs and knocked on your dressing room door but there was no reply. I waited around near the stage hoping you would appear but when I saw the stagehands were all going home I asked them whether they knew where you were and they said that you had gone a long time ago. So I left. Then found I'd missed the last omnibus home and I didn't have enough money with me for a cab.' She was gabbling now and was powerless to stop the tears from pouring down her cheeks. 'But Mr Houghton came out and loaned me the money.' A small sob escaped her lips.

Well, that was *her* done for. Mr Barrett hated offstage dramatics. She groped in her bag for her handkerchief.

Barrett became thoughtful for a moment then he held up his right hand and nodded. 'I realize that some people think it's amusing to bait newcomers,' he admitted. 'I apologize on behalf of the company.' He pulled a large white hankie from his vest pocket and handed it to her.

He believed her!

'If I had wanted to speak to you,' he said kindly, 'it would have been to say how well you had done learning the part so quickly and playing it so well.'

At that the tears and sobs came in a rush. Her whole body shook.

Barrett looked concerned.

'If you get another note either speak to me about it if possible or ignore it unless it has this symbol after the signature. He drew a diamond with W.B. inside it and showed it to Rosa. 'Got that?'

She nodded.

He tore the piece of paper into tiny pieces and threw them in the wastepaper basket.

'And never go wandering backstage after the performance. You could fall down a trap or into machinery in the darkness. In fact from now on, all you ladies must make sure that you leave the theatre together.'

Rosa nodded and smiled tremulously.

She was still to tread the stage as Master Shakespeare Jarvis and might yet play a warm-hearted gypsy woman in *The Romany Rye*.

Life was sweet again.

*   *   *

110

The name Somers Town evoked visions of a place of rural delights and no little size. It was neither.

Somers Town was a small, blunted triangle of land sandwiched between St Pancras Railway Station and Goods Sheds and the Hampstead Road and lying directly to the north of elegant, gated, Bloomsbury. At its centre sat another railway station: Euston.

Back in 1784 one Lord Somers had leased his pastures to a Frenchman who planned to build a pleasant suburb on them but the well-to-do had proved unwilling to cross to the north side of the New Road and the project had failed.

Eventually, the working classes moved into the half-built houses. They were joined by hordes of refugees from the French Revolution and, later, the Spanish uprising of the 1820s. All these inhabitants were poor. As were the parents of Charles Dickens when they lived briefly in Somers Town in 1824. Soon, much of the area degenerated into the worst of slums.

Then came the railways.

The London & Birmingham, the Midland and the Great Northern all decided that the New Road at Somers Town and King's Cross would make ideal venues for their London termini.

After all, to stray further south into the land of the wealthy and influential would not only cost a great deal more but also face implacable opposition.

Those poor rendered homeless by these railway stations and their attendant tracks, train sheds, goods yards, coal drops and hotels, were crammed into the remaining, already crowded, dwellings.

Their extreme deprivation eventually led to some action being taken by the Metropolitan Association for Improving the Dwellings of the Industrious Classes.

A block of flats was built, the very first in London. *The Times* declared them to be of such splendour that an Oxford student might find himself at home in any one of the bedrooms or parlours. But then Oxford students didn't have large, poverty-stricken families. The flats were not a success.

Nonetheless, further blocks of flats for the working classes followed in Somers Town and surrounding areas: King's Cross, Islington and even down in Bloomsbury. These were more successful although, by then, many of the displaced had been forced to move elsewhere.

As a consequence, by the time Sergeant John George Smith went to a Somers Town tenement in search of Miss Gibbons's parents, many of the flats were occupied by railway workers; the Midland Railway had acquired another huge chunk of land thereabouts for their new goods sheds and New Road had metamorphosed into the Euston Road.

Twenty-Two

The gritty London streets were even grittier in Somers Town, where, each day, dozens of railway engines belched their smoke into the air, strewing every surface with greasy coal dust and blocking out much of the sky.

Smith quickened his stride along Ossulston Street in an attempt to keep warm. When he left home it had been one of those shall I/shan't I wear an overcoat days. Now, he realized, as the autumn nip sharpened, that the answer should have been in the positive. But as he had only a heavy winter coat, at this time of year he tended to be either chilled or baked anyway.

St Pancras Buildings turned out to be a monolithic five-storey structure of brick and stucco. Although plain of face it stood out among the decaying Georgian houses as being quite pristine and substantial.

Smith was familiar with such worker housing edifices, so soon found his way to the back where the galleried entrances to the flats were ranged three sides around a courtyard.

Here, groups of children were skipping, playing hopscotch, sailing back and forth on swings or turning giddily on roundabouts. Some were better dressed than others and even wore shoes or boots.

Smith had always been good with children, coming as he did from a large family headed by a widowed mother. When he married Bessie, he inherited three of hers. He was now also a proud father of a son of his own, a two-year-old whom he'd called Arthur Ernest after his late father and Best.

He grinned at the children on the swings and gave each a push that sent them up into the air squealing with delight.

As he did so, he looked up at the flats, where an iron balcony fronted every front door, and acknowledged that he was only delaying his unpleasant task.

He left the roundabout spinning from a lusty heave, took a deep breath, then made his way up to number 14 on the second floor.

Mr and Mrs Gibbons sat very close to each other on the horse-hair sofa, grasping each other's hands tightly. Andrew Gibbons was a tall man with chiselled features who held himself erect; Bertha was delicate and fair with startlingly blue eyes in a waif-like face. Judging from her photograph, Esther's looks had been a fortuitous combination of the two. His fine features and her delicacy.

Red-rimmed eyes and dazed expressions spoke of the couple's uncomprehending grief but they had insisted they were more than willing to answer Smith's questions. Indeed, they seemed eager to talk about their youngest daughter, Esther. A not unusual reaction.

Smith hated interviewing a victim's grieving family. He knew that to lose your child must be to suffer one of the worst blows life can aim at you and felt like a vulture preying over a corpse.

But Best said that to become incoherent with embarrass-ment at the task was both unprofessional and selfish. 'It means you're thinking about your own feelings rather than theirs. Just be prepared, be sympathetic. Then get on with it.'

A great many actresses came from theatrical families partly because, up until recently, for a respectable girl to go into the profession voluntarily had been tantamount to declaring herself a loose woman. To become an actress was to sacrifice your reputation.

The other reason was that girls in theatrical families tended to go on stage early instead of being sent away to school like the boys.

Esther Gibbons had clearly not been of theatrical stock unless her father had been acting when he posed for the photograph on their mantelpiece. It showed him standing before a Jenny Lind No.45 class engine proudly resplendent in the smart uniform of a Midland Railway guard.

Smith began at the beginning, as Best had instructed him to do. He enquired just how it was that Esther had come to be on the stage and playing such a prominent role in a West End success.

Even now there was a hint of pride in their faces as they looked at each other, forming their answers and deciding who was to speak first.

They began speaking together then Andrew Gibbons left off to allow Bertha to say softly, 'Esther always wanted to go on stage.' She smiled sadly at the remembrance. 'She was always the first to get up and sing at family parties and school concerts, wasn't she, Andy?'

Gibbons nodded, his eyes never leaving her face.

'Then we took her and her sister to see *Masks and Faces* at the Prince of Wales and that was that. Before we knew it she had the rest of them acting out theatricals, all done up in my clothes, bedspreads and even, if they got the chance, bits of their father's uniform.'

Tears sprang into her eyes and she looked away.

'We had six other children,' put in Andrew Gibbons, 'three boys and two girls, but we lost one of the boys to tuberculosis and one of the girls to scarlet fever.'

'When she left school Esther got taken on as a trainee lady telegrapher for the company,' her mother continued.

'Good jobs for a woman, them,' put in Andrew.

'Yes. But she didn't like it much so she began to save up to go to voice classes and take dancing lessons.'

'Course, we helped her out a bit when I got some overtime,' added Mr Gibbons.

They went on to describe how Esther began the rounds of the theatrical agencies. Without any stage experience this apparently became even more painful and dispiriting for her than it had been for Rosa de la Drake.

Fate took a hand when the writer and playwright Mr George R. Sims decided to go on one of his pedestrian excursions. The guard on his early morning train on this occasion turned out to be none other than Andrew Gibbons.

As was his practice, Sims asked the guard about his work. When they had been chatting for a while Gibbons seized the opportunity to tell him about Esther's progress or rather lack of it and ask his advice.

'He was very kind,' said Andrew, 'and told me to send her around to see Mr Gooch, who was the manager at Princess's at the time, and that *he* would be able to tell if she had the right spark in her.'

'Mr Gooch liked her,' said Mrs Gibbons, taking up the story, 'but said she must get some experience. He gave her a little work as a super.'

The upshot was that young Esther, at a mere sixteen years of age, began playing some small utility parts and, eventually, won the role of Shakespeare Jarvis in *The Lights o' London*.

'Mr Barrett said she had the right mixture of spirit and propriety,' said Bertha Gibbons.

'Why didn't you report her missing?' Smith broke in, acting on Best's principle of taking people by surprise.

'I did,' said Bertha.

Smith raised his eyebrows. 'But, I thought—'

'Not on the first night,' she admitted. 'Andy was at work – gone up to Glasgow and I was worried when she didn't come home, course I was, but I thought she must be at one of them all-night rehearsals.'

Smith frowned.

'She'd got another part?'

'Oh, no. But she was hoping to get one in Mr Sims's new play, *The Romany Rye*, and I thought that might be what had happened.' Her eyes were filling up with tears and her voice fading to a whisper.

'Or they could have been going over something in the present one,' said Andrew, taking over. 'They do that if bits of it are not going right or they want to change things.'

Bertha was sobbing now. 'If I,' she managed to say, 'if I had reported her missing on that first night would she . . . ?' She couldn't finish the sentence. Andrew put his arms around her and held her.

Smith took a deep breath. 'No,' he said firmly. 'I'm sure it would have made no difference at all.'

He and Andrew Gibbons exchanged glances. Gibbons's expression signalled that he knew that Smith probably had no idea whether it would have made any difference but was grateful to him for the lie.

Mrs Gibbons pulled herself up out of her husband's arms and sat up, dried her eyes and carried on where she had left off.

'When she didn't come home the next day I went down to the theatre and they said she hadn't turned up the night before, so I went to the police. But when I told them she was an actress they didn't seem very interested. Said she had probably gone off with some stage-door lounger. But she wasn't a flighty girl,' insisted Mrs Gibbons, tears overwhelming her again. 'She was a good girl.'

'Had she a gentleman friend?'

Bertha shook her head.

'What about Jerry,' put in Mr Gibbons.

Bertha shrugged. 'He wasn't her boyfriend, really. She'd known him all her life,' she explained to Smith. 'They went to school together.'

Andrew was not to be shifted from his opinion. 'They were sweethearts.'

'*He* thought they were.'

Ah. Something interesting here.

'But she didn't?'

Mrs Gibbons shook her head again. 'She was fond of him and she knew he was very sweet on her.'

'His name is Jerry what?'

'Banks,' said Andrew.

'And where does this Jerry Banks live?'

'Down Ossulston Street.'

'Does he work for the railways?'

Gibbons nodded. 'He's a van boy on Great North Eastern's light parcels. Didn't want to go on the trains because he wanted to stay near Esther.'

'And because he likes horses better than trains and doesn't want to be away from home,' Bertha put in. This sounded like the rehash of an old argument.

So, Jerry rode the railway horse-vans. It was a long-standing joke in the Metropolitan Police that the railways, once heralded as the death knell of horse-drawn traffic, now owned huge numbers of horse-drawn vehicles.

Their open wagons, drays, timber carts, light and heavy parcel vans and express delivery carriages helped clog up London's streets and were a menace with their constant stopping and starting.

Smith had seen many a lad riding the tailboard of a light parcels delivery van, clinging on to its 90-degree slope by a knotted rope and sometimes falling off and rolling in the dirt and getting injured.

Might it be that an aspiring West End actress found such a job undignified?

Had Esther rejected him?

'Always concentrate on the most obvious suspects first,' Best said. 'Especially the rejected lover. Men hate being rejected. It makes them angry.'

And how would Jerry feel about Esther becoming the focus of all male eyes in her tight breeches? It seemed to him that Jerry Banks had the makings of an obvious suspect.

'What is his route?' Smith enquired, trying to hide his excitement.

Gibbons paused then said slowly, 'The West End,' then added, 'But he wouldn't harm our Esther.'

One person whom Best had missed in his 'chats' so far was E. S. Willard, the man who played the dastardly Clifford Armytage in *The Lights o' London*.

The actor was looked upon as something of an enigma, apparently having come from nowhere to land a leading role on the London stage. One in which he had made quite an impression.

Recalling Willard's coldly sneering performance as the black-hearted gentleman villain, Best was mildly disconcerted to discover that in real life not only was he an amiable fellow but that his long, curly moustache had lost some of its length and all of its curl.

During the interviews conducted directly after the death of Talisman, Willard had appeared as puzzled as they as to what had happened to the pistol after it had been wrested from him by the hero. He declared that he had detected no difference in its weight or feel that night and confirmed that it had been delivered to him by the call boy, as usual. He knew nothing about Talisman.

As for Esther's death, he was as shocked as the rest of them. More so, even.

'She seemed such a nice, unspoiled girl and so excited to get this opportunity. I'm very shocked,' he told Best as they sat in the circle bar after the matinee performance.

Best wondered aloud why he had not heard of him, Willard, before his sudden rise to prominence, pointing out that he appeared to have come upon the scene from nowhere.

Willard laughed. 'Like a genie from a bottle!' He gave a rueful grin. 'No. I've been here before – back in '75 for a couple of productions. I already had my spurs even then. I'd done six years in the provinces, the last few in leading roles. But – ' he shrugged – 'I soon learned that the opportunities to play leading roles in the capital were, shall we say, somewhat limited.'

'Actor-managers?' asked Best.

He nodded. 'All powerful, egotistical, self-serving creatures to a man.' He took a deep breath. 'You might say, I was disillusioned. So I went touring – playing lead roles.'

Very outspoken. That can't have gone down well with London managements.

'But you came back?'

He nodded. 'Wilson Barrett invited me and I'd heard he was a bit of an exception among the breed.' He paused and sighed. 'Besides, touring becomes very tiring!' He laughed.

118

'There you have it – my sad story!'

But while Willard had made a splash with his role it was not *exactly* the lead. Meaty and dramatic perhaps. But not the lead. The actor-manager had that.

Had he been disappointed after all? Best could find nothing suspicious about the man other than the possibility of some chagrin and the fact that the gun had been in his charge before being handed on.

He had to admit that Willard was a charming person.

They all were.

And none of them showed any signs of guilt.

But then, they were actors, weren't they?

Twenty-Three

Two people were vying for Best's attention as he finished talking to E. S. Willard. One was a ferrety little man, cap in hand. The other was Detective Sergeant John George Smith.

Best chose the ferrety man and held up his hand to an eager Smith saying, 'Won't be long, John George, if my guess is correct.'

His guess was that judging by the puffy-faced pallor, shaven head and ill-fitting 'lunatic suit', the man was a recently released ex-con with information to sell. He had not yet even had the time for his hair to grow a little or to get himself a better suit from a prisoners' aid mission. The cons always complained that the prison release issue was just like the garb given to the inmates of lunatic asylums and usually couldn't wait to shed it.

The man introduced himself as Ginger Barnet, which was a bit of a joke. Best could see the reason for the 'Ginger' nickname from the light fuzz on his head but barnet was slang for hair (Cockney rhyming: Barnet Fair). So either Ginger was being a bit cheeky or was stupid enough to give only his nickname. No matter. Like the costers, some prisoners became more familiar with their nicknames than their real ones.

At Ginger's next words Best brightened.

'Basher Carter give me a message for you.'

There was a pause.

'Well, what is it?' asked Best as he reached into his right-hand trouser pocket to pull out a handful of coin.

Ginger looked at the money expectantly. Best looked back at him until the man realized that he was not going to give any of it away until he had some idea what was on offer.

'He says he knows where Morris Little is.'

Best's spirit soared although his face remained impassive. News of the third band boy, at last. 'And where's that?'

Ginger shook his head. 'Dunno. You got to go to see him and he'll tell you.'

The man's eyes remained on the money.

'I see.'

'He said you'd see me all right if I came right off – I walked straight here from Holloway and . . .'

Best knew that this could be just a con. Ginger might have learned from Carter that Best was desperate to know the whereabouts of Little. There were ways around the silent system. He took a shilling from the pile.

'Right. Take this and come back tomorrow. 'If you are telling the truth, there'll be more.'

The man hesitated, disappointed. Then he grabbed the shilling, saying, 'He says he'll need privileges.'

That sounded like Carter. Best relented and added another shilling.

Of course, Carter could also be conning him. Prisoners would do anything to get time off from the treadmill, a few cigarettes and a bit of unrestricted conversation.

When John George finally got to speak to Best he was beside himself with impatience.

'Jerry Banks,' he broke out, 'is a very obvious suspect.'

'Never heard of him,' said Best teasingly.

120

'Esther's boyfriend. At least that's what her father says but her mother says he wasn't,' Smith added in a rush.

'Have a drink,' said Best. 'You're off duty now, or should be.' He pointed to a barstool and ordered a pint of Alsops Ale.

When Smith had poured out his news about the might, might-not-be swain of the victim, Best nodded his head approvingly.

'That's good,' he said. 'Very good. You did well.'

This was less than Smith had expected. He'd imagined Best being cock-a-hoop at having the killer in his sights at last. Best had been more excited by the news given him by that little runt of a man. He hadn't shown it but Smith could tell.

'But don't you see – it's probably him! Jealous, enraged at seeing her flaunting herself on stage. Thinking he was losing her—'

'That's all a bit of an assumption,' said Best. 'Considering we've not even laid eyes on the fellow yet.' He noticed Smith's disappointment, 'But it's very promising, I'll grant you. Well worth lots more looking into.' He paused. 'How might Talisman fit into this, d'you think?'

Momentarily Smith was stumped.

'Er . . .'

He'd clearly not given this idea much, if any, thought. Best was always encouraging him – think further. Don't rely on me to sort out what it all means.

He did think now, sucking in his lips in concentration. Inspiration suddenly struck and he exclaimed, 'Him and Esther might have been having a romance. Or – or Jerry thought they were!'

'Hmm,' mused Best. 'So you reckon that even though she didn't want a van boy as a sweetheart she might settle for a lowly super?'

'You never know,' said Smith, 'when it comes to love. Look at me and Bessie.' Smith had ended up marrying the widow of a suspect turned murder victim from their first case together.

'True,' said Best. 'I can't argue with that. Well, go to it then. Find Jerry Banks while I go to see my jailbird friend.'

121

He touched his glass to Smith's. 'Good luck to both of us. We certainly need it.'

It had taken some time and some hard bargaining but Carter eventually gave the information Best had come for.

''E's in the band at the Oxford.'

Best frowned. 'But we've been there.'

The Oxford was a very successful music hall at the eastern end of Oxford Street, where it met Tottenham Court Road.

''E's changed 'is name. Calls hisself Jones now, Hector Jones.'

'Why's that?'

'Dunno. Maybe 'e's been up to something as he shouldn't.' He grinned. 'Don't recall 'e was a naughty boy – but things change, don't they?'

'How do you know this?'

'Mutual acquaintance told me.'

'Just recently.'

Carter grinned. 'Yeah.'

And that was it.

I might have been conned, thought Best, but I don't think so.

Probably knew all along and had been stringing me along. No matter, if it was good information it meant some progress at last.

The Oxford's newest acts were running through their performances so that the ASM could note their exact duration in his Time Book and the band become familiar with their music.

There was no chance of interrupting the proceedings. Not if Best wanted the co-operation of Morris Little. Putting him in everyone's bad books by holding them up would scarcely achieve that. No matter, he'd been told that they were going to break in about ten minutes 'for the necessary', so Best just sat back in the stalls and watched the turns.

As he'd come in, a moderately amusing serio-comic had been performing. Now, after a pause, two demure young misses came on to a light refrain with a hint of a march to it.

Their very proper black gowns concealed every suspicion of flesh apart from that of their faces. They were framed by dark bonnets with white frills. Each carried a stout umbrella and a bag from which a newspapers peeped just far enough for you to see the title writ very large, WAR CRY!

At first they held their eyes down in a mock shy manner then raised them slowly as they introduced themselves in song:

'*They call me Happy Eliza,*' explained one.

'*And me Converted Jane,*' chimed in the other.

Their voices joined to sing with feigned shame, '*We've been so wicked in our time, we'll never do so again!*'

Their voices gathered power and momentum.

'*Oh will you come and join us, it's so easily understood.*'

Then came the climax: '*We're the Hal-le-lujah sisters and we're bound to do you good!*'

At this the orchestra went off into a frenzy of tambourine rattling and cymbal clashing.

Best grinned. These must be the Sisters Cuthbert that Littlechild had told him about. They were the latest popular novelty act at the Crystal Palace and on the halls.

While adopting their style – 'Why should the devil have all the best tunes?' their founder William Booth had asked – the 'Sallies' attacked the drinking and prostitution that went on at the music halls.

An act at the Oxford taking the rise out of the Army's 'Hallelujah Lassies' was a particularly cheeky and ironic gesture given the theatre's past reputation.

At one time this music hall had been a favourite haunt of the male gentry with the result that the female part of the audience became exclusively composed of ladies of the night and family audiences shunned the place. The management made the mistake of playing up to this clientele by providing some lewd entertainment – which got them shut down.

Now, they played to the usual working-class family audience.

When the band finally took their break and began moving away from the orchestra pit, Best noticed the ASM bending over the drummer and pointing towards the stalls.

123

Shortly afterwards, Hector Jones appeared beside him. He had a wary look in his small, dark eyes and a none-too-pleased expression on his rather florid face. His head of black, springy, curls and his stocky build gave him the look of a Welsh poet, a suspicious Welsh poet.

Best moved along one and indicated the seat beside him. Jones remained standing.

'What's all this about?' he asked in a tone which managed to stay reasonably polite but at the same time was verging on the aggressive. 'I don't have much time to spare.'

'Neither do I,' rejoined Best coldly. He fixed the bandsman with an I'm-not-to-be-trifled-with expression and said, 'It's important that I have a short conversation with you *now*. Then, if I deem it necessary, I will arrange to meet you again so we can talk further.'

Jones stared at him for a moment, clearly deciding what would be his next best move. Best settled the matter with a brisk, 'Look, it's that or we can go down to the police station *now*, where a possibly much more extended conversation will take place.'

It was all bluff of course. He had no grounds to arrest the man except, perhaps, for obstructing the police in the execution of their duty and that would be stretching it a little. In his favour, however, was the fact that the music halls liked to avoid any 'trouble with the police' and Jones would know that.

To his surprise Jones nodded, sighed wearily and sat down heavily next to Best.

'It's about Talisman, isn't it?'

'Yes.'

'And I thought I was free of the man now.'

Best did his utmost to keep the surprise from his face and to hold his eyebrows down. Was this to be one of those sudden, instant confessions spilled out by someone who'd been worried to distraction about getting caught, then relieved when the police finally found them?

Either that, or Jones was being foolishly outspoken. Or he had an unbreakable alibi.

'The man was a trial to you?'

Jones shook his head in disbelief at his own bad luck. 'That's putting it mild. Couldn't help it, poor soul, I suppose. God rest his soul now, but . . .'

'You'd better tell me all about it.'

Twenty-Four

'Talisman was very timid when we was at the Foundling home, and you know nothing gets a bully goin' more than a timid boy,' said Jones.

Best nodded. 'Carter said you used to protect him.'

'Ah, Carter. So you've seen him?'

'Yes.'

'How's *he* doin' these days?' Jones gave a knowing half-smile.

'Not well.'

'He's inside?'

Best nodded.

'Bound to happen, I suppose.' Jones grimaced. 'Always a wrong un, that one.'

'So,' said Best, bringing them back to the subject, 'you protected Talisman?'

'Yes.' He paused, then explained. 'Bit strange but he sort of reminded me of my foster sister Jeannie. I'd always stuck up for her but when we came to the home she was sent to the girls' part of the home and we never saw each other again.' He paused. 'I s'pose I got quite fond of Talisman because of that really. You know, you need all the affection you can get in an orphanage.'

'Understandably.'

Best noticed that he had used the word affection rather than love.

'I have to admit that I was quite set up about him taking a

125

shine to me – at first. But, of course, he began to cling. Everywhere I went he was there. It wasn't so bad at the home – we were in separate classes and we slept in different wards but it drove me crazy after we joined the army. Couldn't move without him.'

As he spoke Jones was clasping and unclasping his hands.

'You signed on together though?'

'Oh, yeah. But he only joined because I did. I knew it would be a terrible place for the likes of him and I tried to tell him but he wouldn't listen.' He looked thoughtful. 'He was weak but he was stubborn an' all.' The hand-wringing was stepping up a pace.

'It got harder for me. We were in the same band and slept in the same barracks. At first I didn't mind because we knew nobody and all three of us clung together.' He stopped to explain. 'You see, us being Foundling boys we didn't know how to mix with people outside. But, in the end, because I was a good drummer I started to make new friends among the other lads who wanted to learn how to do it.'

Jones locked his bunched fingers together and pulled as if trying to prise them apart.

'He got jealous.'

'How did that show?'

'Like with a woman. Sulks. Flares of temper.'

'Violence?'

'Oh, no. Never. Might have been easier if it had. Would have been less embarrassing if I could have punched him on the nose, wouldn't it?' He paused before saying, 'He wasn't happy about my family either.'

'Family?'

Jones nodded. 'My foster parents found me when I was grown.'

'I didn't know they could.'

'Oh, aye. When you're grown up – if they want – can't do it the other way around. If it's just *you* wants to find *them*.'

The orchestra was starting to reassemble and Jones glanced over at them worriedly.

'So,' said Best to hurry things on, 'you left the army and he did too?'

126

Jones nodded. 'Followed me out. I got a job at the Princess's and thought – well, he can't follow me here because there's no more vacancies.' The hand-wringing became acute. 'But he started coming there as a super whenever he could. It was very embarrassing.' Jones became agitated. 'I told him it was all over – that I was married now and—' He stopped suddenly and looked aghast at what he had just blurted out.

'So, then,' said Best, giving him a blankly encouraging smile as if he hadn't recognized the portent of what the man had said. He'd already realized that the pair had probably been lovers at some time.

After all, homosexuality was rife in public schools – why not orphanages? Even more reason for it there with all those boys desperate for affection. But he wasn't interested in prosecuting Jones, even if he was able to prove the offence that could carry a life sentence. Anyway, Talisman was dead.

'So, then,' said Jones eventually, 'I decided that there was nothing for it but to get another job, change my professional name and alter my appearance best I could.' He smiled wanly and pulled at one of his curly locks. 'I didn't always look like one of those aesthetes.'

Best was perplexed.

'But the Oxford is in the same street as the Princess's. He could have bumped into you at any time.'

The orchestra leader was signalling to Jones. He waved back and stood up. Best extended his hand and spread his fingers to indicate give me five minutes. The leader nodded and they began tuning up.

'I didn't come here at first,' explained Jones. 'Went to the Pavilion but then I got a better offer here and with the times of performances being different and everything I thought it would be OK.'

'And was it?'

He seemed to be about to say something then changed his mind and said, 'Yeah. Yeah,' hurriedly and rather unconvincingly. 'It worked.'

'Just two more quick questions for now.'

'Yeah?'

'Had Talisman any enemies you know of?'

He shook his head. 'None. Most people didn't even notice him.'

That was certainly true.

'Have you any idea who might want to kill him?'

'Not a clue,' said Jones, looking towards the orchestra pit and starting to move.

Neither have I, thought Best as he waved the man away.

The Great North Eastern Railway had been accused of building a passenger terminal at King's Cross that was quite inadequate for its growing use. Not so their fifty-nine-acre goods yard situated about a third of a mile to the north.

Scattered across a canal-side site which could have accommodated a large village were warehouses, engine sheds and turntables, coal drops, warehouses, stone docks, and stables enough to accommodate 1,500 horses. All the farm produce from the fertile eastern England poured in here, particularly potatoes. Also fish and coal and much else.

There wouldn't be so much talk about the grand passenger stations if people came to see this, thought Smith. But then, of course, they couldn't – except from a distance. As with the Thames-side docks, railway goods yards were closed to the general public.

Despite the continuing autumnal chill, Smith paused for a moment on Somers Bridge to watch the frantic activity around the Granary; the largest and most important building in the Yard.

While its façade was plain, the six-storey Granary was, by its sheer size and solidity, more impressive and monumental than King's Cross passenger terminal.

A melee of carts, drays and vans jostled for space under the numerous hoists, which doled out at the front what had been fed into the back by an endless flow of goods trains.

Canal boats even passed in and out of the building via specially built tunnels which led into the basement.

The goods office alongside the Granary was, by contrast, a plain little brick building and Harding, the sharp-faced luggage and light parcels clerk, was no nonsense too.

'He's gone,' he said peremptorily when Smith enquired the whereabouts of Jerry Banks.

'On his rounds?' asked Smith.

'No. He's left. Disappeared. Scarpered.'

'When?'

'The day before yesterday. Halfway through his round he just got off to deliver a parcel – and didn't come back. We ain't seen him since.'

'Where was he delivering?'

'Dunno.'

'Here, I'm losing time!' exclaimed a van driver waiting behind Smith.

Harding turned to a bank of pigeonholes and took a sheet of paper from one of them. Smith stood back so that the muttering man could be dealt with but when several more drivers appeared, he reclaimed his position and asked, 'Who would know where they were at the time?'

'The van man.'

'Where's he now?'

'On his rounds, course.'

'Give me his route for today.'

'Oh, for gawd's sake!'

Smith's still youthful looks could operate against him when dealing with the likes of Harding. It was time to assert himself.

He took a deep breath, pulled himself up to his full six feet, assumed a severe expression quite alien to his nature and commanded slowly and menacingly, *'Tell me his route.'*

The man complied.

Smith wasn't certain whether it mattered a jot just where Jerry Banks had been when he had taken abrupt leave of his post but the young sergeant was trying to think beyond, as instructed by Best.

Maybe he *had* begun to rely too much on the Detective Inspector to sort out the meaning of everything. Just taking him the information he had collected, like a retriever on a shoot, then standing back, waiting to be thrown a scrap of praise and enlightenment?

Nonetheless, when he *did* reach a conclusion Best had not always appreciated it.

But now he might realize that I was right all along, thought Smith, when I said that Jerry Banks was a very likely suspect.

129

Twenty-Five

This time no ferrety ex-jailbird competed for Best's attention. Instead he was deep in conversation with Smart, the Super Master.

These days the man's response to Best's questions ranged from the resentful to the effusive but was always co-operative.

That had been his attitude since Best had threatened to close the theatre down if he didn't answer his questions while also revealing that he knew about the man's heavy drinking.

Smart's strange see-sawing between cryptic answers and sudden gushes of excessive information gave Best the feeling that there were two characters inside the man fighting to get out. Neither won. Neither of them was very attractive.

But the Smart who gushed was most likely to be of use if only Best could keep his own attention sufficiently riveted so as to recognize the more valuable nuggets of information when they emerged.

Best had asked the man whether he knew members of the band and this had set him off on a tirade about how uncouth musicians were and how messy in their habits.

Apparently, they left half drunk cups of tea and cigarette ends all over the place. Best couldn't see what difference this could make to Smart since he was neither a cleaner nor the manager.

But the DI had grasped that his best strategy was to hear out the Super Master's gripes, then slip in a pertinent question. So when Smart began naming the band's worst offenders he asked quickly, 'So you know individual members of the band, do you?'

130

'Some of them, course. Specially those that have been here a long time. Most just by sight of course.'

'Did you know Morris Little?'

'That drummer? Yeah. He just got up and left one day, the leader said. He was furious. No warning or nothing. Some of your lot must have been after him, I reckon.'

'He's playing at the Oxford,' said Best, who saw no harm in letting it out now. Could cause a bit of gossip and that might be fruitful.

'Oh, he is, is he?' said Smart. 'More money, course, but nothing like the turns get.' Bit of a sore point this, Best had heard.

'Well, they don't have to dash about from hall to hall like the performers do,' said Best. Indeed he knew that some of the popular performers died young from the strain of it all but their places were quickly filled by other hopefuls.

'They all wants to get in on it now,' grumbled Smart. 'I'm always catching the supers practising little dances and singing stupid little songs in the hope of getting on the halls.'

'Have you seen Little recently?' asked Best casually.

Smart shook his head. 'Nah,' he shrugged. Then said, 'Wait a minute though, I did hear something about him just the other day.' He tried to think. 'Yeah, that's right – someone said how he'd been around to collect something and that he looked different and . . .'

Smith was hovering, desperately trying to attract Best's attention. Best saw him and signalled him to wait but the young sergeant couldn't stop himself. He pushed in, insisting, 'Got to speak to you, sir.'

Best was not pleased. He sensed he had just been about to get some vital information. He excused himself from Smart, who took the opportunity to rush off, muttering and grasping his clipboard to his scrawny chest.

'This better be important,' Best hissed.

Smith gulped but spilled out, 'It is! It is! Jerry Banks has gone missing!'

Best considered this for a moment while he cooled down and finally agreed, 'Yes, it is important.'

Smith sighed with relief and rushed on, 'He went off to

deliver a parcel the day before yesterday and never came back.'

'Where was he delivering?'

'Don't know, yet.'

'Time?'

'Don't know, yet.'

'State of mind?'

'Don't know that either – yet.' Must remember to ask that, he thought. 'Only his van man would know all that and he was out on his rounds. I've got his delivery roster for today.' He thrust it towards Best, like a small boy showing his mother his school drawings.

Best raised one eyebrow, put his head to one side and grinned.

Smith pulled the worksheet back, sheepishly returned Best's grin and said, 'He comes round here. I reckon he won't have reached Oxford Street yet – the traffic is terrible out there. There's been an accident – a cart and an omnibus. So I thought I'd better just let you know before I went out to catch him.'

Best nodded. 'Right, you did well.' He paused. 'So, what do you make of all this, John George?'

'Well, of course, Banks might have done the murder and gone on the run when he heard the body had been found.'

'Of course. Or . . .'

Smith had been giving this matter some thought en route and while walking down Tottenham Court Road after he had been obliged to get off the omnibus following the accident. 'He might have suspected who done it and gone after them.'

'Yes. Excellent.' Best kept his eyes on his young protégé willing him to think for himself. 'Or . . .'

Smith hesitated, and began looking about him and up into the corner of the auditorium's ornate ceiling as though the elaborate curlicues up there might assist him. It came to him in a flash. Obvious really. 'He might have gone off to kill himself because his heart was broken.'

Best smiled. The lad was such a romantic. But then, so was he.

'Correct. Which is why we need to know where he was –

by the Regent's Canal or the Thames or wherever.' Best pointed out towards Oxford Street. 'Go find your van man.'

It was late evening and Helen was still working at her easel when Best got home. He was torn between wishing she didn't work so hard and being happy that she had something with which to occupy herself while he was kept late at times like these.

In any case she always reminded him that if they couldn't afford to pay Bessie to cook and Mary to clean she would have to work much harder. If you want to see hard work, she would say, watch a woman on washday. She bends over a steaming boiler, lifts out heavy, wet clothes and bed linen then carries heavy baskets of them out to the garden to peg out on the line. That's hard work, she would say.

Best remembered his mother doing just that. She was always worn out and weary on washday, which, for some reason, was always on a Monday. Only she hung her washing up in a sooty East End backyard, not a garden in Notting Hill.

Instead of all this domestic toil, there was Helen placing highlights on to her dramatic oil of St Nicholas Church in Newcastle upon Tyne.

'Bit of artistic licence there,' he teased, slipping his arms up under her smock to encircle her waist. 'The sun never penetrated through that murky atmosphere!'

She half turned and planted a highlight on his nose. 'Impertinence. Yes, it did – when the wind was in the right direction.'

They both smiled. They had been reunited in the church after a long separation, but Newcastle was also where he had almost lost her for good.

He hugged her tighter. She pushed him away, laid aside her brush, removed her smock and kissed him passionately, then looked at her brushes and sighed.

'I know,' he said, 'you have to clean them.'

He removed his jacket and rolled up his sleeves while she poured out two dishes of turpentine. They talked about the case as they began dipping the brushes one by one into the liquid, working them up and down, watching captive paint seep out in an oddly satisfying manner.

He made her smile with his efforts to make John George think for himself.

'You're his replacement father,' she laughed. 'Of course he brings all his toys to you to admire and to make them work!'

'Hmph. He's not going to get much further until he starts thinking for himself.'

'I think he's better than you give him credit for,' she insisted. She'd always had a soft spot for Smith ever since they united in a desperate search for Best when they found he had been aboard the ill-fated pleasure steamer the *Princess Alice*. 'He'd be better still if he got away from you.'

'Oh!' Best was shocked. 'I don't think that's necessary.'

'I know you don't. But it might help *him*.'

He didn't comment on that. She knew him too well. She was saddened to hear about Jerry Banks.

'Question is,' said Best, 'did he go on the run because he did it and heard about them finding the body? Or did he find out she was dead and get so upset he ran off blindly?'

'Might have thought he'd be blamed anyway.'

'Yes, there is that.'

'I expect he's committed suicide,' she said, handing him another brush to dip and pummel.

He stopped, holding the brush aloft.

'How odd you should come to that conclusion straight away. It was the third solution John George thought of and that took some prising out of him.'

'I'm older,' she replied. 'The very idea of doing away with yourself is too unbelievable to young people – unless they've been in desperate situations themselves. And you're more experienced than John George. Much more. Remember that.'

'I suppose.'

She waited until he had finished with the last brush, gathered them up and took them over to the sink in the corner of the studio. Then she turned on the tap and began rubbing the brushes with soap.

'If Jerry Banks *didn't* kill her it doesn't make sense him going off like that,' said Best.

'Why not?'

'Well, *in my experience* – ' he grinned at her – 'if people hear terrible news like that they are desperate to see the body. Find out exactly what happened.'

'But he's only a boy. News of her death might be enough.' She began handing him the rinsed brushes one by one. He took them in a clean rag and squeezed them to remove the excess water.

'Maybe he went to the Princess's. What did the van man say?'

'He said that Jerry was incoherent when he came back after delivering a parcel to the American Stores at fifty-six Oxford Street.'

Helen raised her eyebrows.

'All right, Jerry was babbling and crying is what the van man *actually* said. He grabbed the next parcel – which was for a photographer's next door at number fifty-seven – went off and didn't come back.'

'Did the van man see where he went?'

'No, he'd moved on a little to the next stop.'

'What number is the Princess's?'

'Seventy-three.'

'A few doors away.'

'No one saw him come in there.'

'Theatres are big places.'

'He'd never get past the stage door man.'

She gave him a sidelong glance.

'Well, all right, he might have. But surely *somebody* would have seen him? The place was alive with coppers.'

'Exactly.'

She was right again. As well as scepticism he'd also taught her that the more people there were at a scene, particularly people supposedly in control, the more no one was.

With all that frantic activity on the day after Emily's body had been found Jerry Banks could easily have slipped in unnoticed.

Helen was too good a student and maybe *he* needed retrospective lessons in thinking for himself. Or a little more sleep? That would be splendid.

'So,' said Best as he placed the last dried brush at the end

135

of a row where they lay like fallen soldiers. 'I've compiled the information for an entry in *The Police Gazette* and telegraphed all stations asking them to keep a lookout.'

That sounded more impressive than it was. In reality 'all stations' meant only divisional headquarters and their inspector's station, the only ones to have electric telegraph machines. It was left to them to see that their other stations received the news that there was a man on the run or a body to be found. Some divisions were quicker at this than others. Some had sparse manpower and large areas to cover – or a lazy inspector.

Suspects had been lost to them for ever due to messages being passed on too late.

Best waxed indignant on the subject but Helen seemed to be only half listening. Perhaps because she had heard it before. It was one of the bees in his bonnet.

Eventually, as she dried her hands, she said slowly, 'You know you were telling me about that young woman who so caught your eye in *It's Never Too Late To Mend*?'

She took his hand and led him over to the sofa.

He nodded, smiling. 'Ida Blackmore.'

Was Helen jealous?

The thought rather pleased him. Normally she gave no hint of such a weakness. Many wives would be worried about him working among beautiful women in the theatre but she'd given no sign of concern.

'Didn't you tell me that she had failed to turn up for a performance one night – and was never seen again?'

'Yes.'

'And this was at the Princess's?'

'Yes.'

'Don't you think there might be some connection?'

He sat down abruptly momentarily startled by the idea. Then he said, 'I don't know about *never seen again.*'

'Have you heard of her since?'

'No, but—'

'And the agent hadn't?'

'No.'

'He'd be in a position to.'

Best shook his head. 'But no body was found – well, not I assume one which was identified as her and I . . .'

He was confused by this new proposition.

'No,' he said, suddenly confident. 'It was just too long ago to be connected. Eighteen sixty-six if I remember rightly. That's *sixteen* years ago. The building was different then. There was another management – and it's such a transient profession – people must just drift away quite often . . .'

'Perhaps,' said Helen in that mildly irritating way of hers which indicated that she was unconvinced but was not going to argue.

'I think,' said Best firmly, 'that maybe John George is right. Jerry Banks is definitely the most likely suspect. Straightforward case of jealousy. As you know, it usually is the boyfriend or husband.'

He realized that he sounded pompous. Was he being so dogmatic because he didn't really believe that?

'Of course,' said Helen.

'Anyway, that's enough of that.' He reached over and silenced her mouth with his.

Twenty-Six

'I have to admit that I have seen Esther and Jerry having rows,' said Mrs Stephens as she undid the ribbons and removed her blue crêpe bonnet.

'Where?'

'At the stage door. She was in tears sometimes afterwards.'

'Did she say what they were about?'

She nodded and dabbed her eyes. 'Mainly that she didn't love Jerry – except like a brother and he wouldn't accept that. He was sure there was someone else.'

'And was there?'

137

'Not that I know of. She had her admirers of course. I used to see some of the supers eyeing her. She was a pretty girl.' The old trouper looked sad as she took up some greasepaint and began applying it to her cheeks in preparation for the matinee performance. 'I liked Esther. She wasn't silly like some of them.'

'Did Jerry object to her being an actress?'

'Oh yes, he thought that was why he had lost her. But in truth he'd never really had her.'

'Was he ever violent towards her?'

She hesitated, rouge puff held to her cheek. 'No, I don't think so. She never mentioned it if he was.' She placed the pad back in the pot. 'To be honest, from what she said, he didn't sound like a violent man. More like a desperate young lad. She was heartbroken at hurting him.'

So, they had rows, heated rows and the boy was desperate to keep her. Who knows how his frustration and anger might suddenly have overtaken him? This certainly qualified Jerry Banks as an even more likely suspect on the run.

Best wondered whether they should print some posters advertising the fact that Jerry was a murder suspect who had taken flight. He'd need to speak to Cheadle and Williamson first to see how much of a reward they thought the Commissioner would approve.

They would probably need more concrete evidence against the lad before they'd agree to that, however. Perhaps someone who had seen him having a row with Esther or just seen them together on the day she went missing. Or, perhaps seen him wearing a jacket with a button missing and tear where it should have been.

Meanwhile, he mentioned the possibility of the reward posters to Ambrose Harcourt, Mr Barrett's dresser, judging that this might be a good way to start the news spreading around.

Gossip winged its way around a theatre at the speed of light and the suggestion of a reward might start jogging memories as well as frightening the murderer.

Lurking at the back of his mind while he was cogitating about Jerry Banks was what Helen had said last night about

Ida Blackmore. It kept coming forward to worry him and he kept sending it back with the excuse that it was too long ago and too unlikely even to consider.

He could be wrong. If he was, the result could be disastrous for another young woman.

Since he was in limbo over both these present cases at the moment he decided that he would try to trace his youthful passion, Ida Blackmore.

Doubtless she would be found out in the suburbs somewhere, surrounded by a large brood of children, and would be astounded that he should imagine otherwise. Doubtless, too, he would look a fool tracing her up like that.

But then, maybe she wasn't. Maybe she was lying in a cold, anonymous grave. He would never forgive himself if she had been murdered and he had done nothing about it.

He would begin by going back to the theatrical agent, Augustus Frobisher, to discover more details about Ida Blackmore's disappearance while she was playing in that sensational play, *It's Never Too Late to Mend*.

It transpired that Ida Blackmore *was* one of the many young actresses who did hail from a theatrical family. As a baby, like the now famous Ellen Terry, Ida had slept wrapped in a shawl in a drawer in her mother's dressing room.

Ellen Terry's stage debut took place in 1856 at the age of nine when she played Mamillius in *The Winter's Tale* at the Princess's during the reign of Charles Kean.

At around the same time, the five-year-old Ida Blackmore had a less auspicious beginning in pantomime in Leeds. She was cast as a fairy whose job it was to distribute Christmas presents, but she made quite an impact in this modest role when, on the first night, she refused to hand over the presents but began to open them herself.

But she did this so winningly and she was such an adorable child that this 'business' was repeated for the rest of the run.

Later, she followed the route of so many actresses by playing a variety of children's roles including lively boys and then progressed to pretending to be various lively young men.

These 'breeches roles' allowed young women a freedom of

movement and expression which they would remember with affection for the rest of their lives after the heavy restrictions of womanhood had long been laid upon them.

It seemed that the Blackmore clan (mother, Edie; father, Rupert; three boys and four girls) had been well known in the provinces, where they had spent most of their lives touring.

At a time when respectable people would not dream of mixing socially with actors, the theatre became the only world Ida and her sister knew and the plays her education. Her brothers, however, had been sent away to boarding schools paid for, in part, by the earnings of the girls.

Best learned all this about Ida and the lives of such young women from her agent, Augustus Frobisher. His interest in the girl had also been reawakened by Best's comments, and this encouraged him to look out and peruse her old file. Like Helen, he also now began to question Ida's fate.

When grown, the other Blackmore children had found their own way either inside or outside the profession. This left their parents, Edie and Rupert, free to accept an offer of a London haven in another 'family', that of the Bancrofts who now ran the Haymarket Theatre. Best headed there next.

Twenty-Seven

It was late afternoon and a heavy fog had already built up by the time Best crossed Oxford Street and made his way into Soho by way of Berwick Street. Here, desperately poor people eked out a miserable existence, crammed into old houses which had been divided off into tenements.

The last of the wealthy folk had long since moved out of Soho and the foreigners, prostitutes and the poor had moved in. The mix gave the area a mildly raffish and exotic air, which tempered the squalor a little, but the courtyards and alleys leading off the streets were dark and sinister.

As the fog thickened, Best trod carefully to avoid stepping blindly into the path of a cart or carriage in the roadway or stepping on to something disgusting on the pavement.

He turned right into Broad Street, his footsteps strangely deadened in the increasing murk drawing itself around him. Even the pathetic streetwalkers who habitually thronged these pavements had started to give up the unequal struggle and retreat indoors.

Realizing he'd been foolish to walk through this area alone in such conditions, Best began peering as far as he could into the murk and listening hard for stealthily approaching footsteps behind him. It's a good job I know my way around here, he thought, or I might get lost and go wandering off into one of those blind alleys where I'd be easy prey. That was still a possibility.

As he turned left into Little Windmill Street, he suddenly felt a hand on his arm. He started, looked down and saw a filthy, shivering, barefoot little girl of about eight years old. She held out her grimy hand.

So much for my acute observation, Best thought as he pulled a three-penny piece from his pocket and placed it into her paw before continuing on into Great Windmill Street.

Soon, to his relief, he was out into the wider streets just east of Regent Circus South where the larger and stronger street lights penetrated further into the gloom.

He found his way straight down the Haymarket, where, despite his being aware of their proximity, the tall white columns of Haymarket Theatre's Grecian portico loomed up suddenly before him. It was a relief to enter the bright, warm and luxurious interior. This was the home of stage royalty – that most eminent of theatre couples – the Bancrofts.

For many years this husband and wife team had led the British theatre's march towards professionalism and respectability.

It had all begun when Mrs Bancroft, then young Marie Wilton, another daughter of a stage family and a burlesque favourite, had become desperate to play comedy. Finding no

141

one prepared to give her the opportunity, she borrowed a thousand pounds and bought her own theatre.

The Queen's in Tottenham Street was not a promising venue, being small, dilapidated and situated well outside fashionable Theatreland.

Undaunted, Marie had the theatre redecorated, renamed it the Prince of Wales and acquired the services of a promising playwright, Thomas William Robertson. She opened the doors to the public in 1865 and began a vogue for English drawing-room comedy and drama to replace the then popular melodrama and endless translations from the French.

Shortly afterwards, she married one of her actors, Squire Bancroft. The pair proved excellent managers, businesslike and meticulous regarding every production detail in an era when much theatre management had become casual and sloppy.

They also brought about many theatre reforms such as paying actors decent wages, providing stage costumes for the actresses, allowing sufficient rehearsal time, introducing a more natural style of acting and gathering fine talent around them. Not least, they were willing to play minor roles when necessary for the good of the production.

As a result, despite its small size and unfashionable situation, the Prince of Wales became one of the most popular theatres in London, even attracting royalty to its doors. The British stage in general grew in status and respectability along with the Bancrofts.

Best had learned all this when their history had been retold in newspapers and magazines on their recent move to the much larger, more centrally placed Theatre Royal in the Haymarket.

The move had inspired much comment and speculation as to whether this new venue might at last prove to be the downfall of the golden pair.

It almost seemed so when the pittites rioted on their opening night because while remodelling the theatre, the Bancrofts had done away with the pit. It was the couple's first experience of public disapproval and shook them somewhat. But things had settled down after they had launched into a series of revivals of previous successes.

Only Squire Bancroft was around, conducting an initial read-through of one of them, entitled *Plot and Passion*. He greeted Best in a friendly fashion, which rather surprised Best, who'd thought he looked a little pompous in an actor-manager photograph he and Helen had seen.

In this, much to Helen's amusement, he sat wearing a top hat and monocle and holding a cigar, looking out at the camera in a suitably imposing fashion. Marie, meanwhile, stood sideways, looking only at him. 'As though he was the architect of it all!' Helen had exclaimed.

Edie and Rupert Blackmore proved to be what even Best recognized as a couple of real old troupers, toughened and made socially adaptable by their many years on the road.

Edie, who looked a little older than her husband, was bouncy and jolly, if a little perplexed by the arrival of a Scotland Yard detective wanting to speak to them. Rupert was a bit more serious and down-to-earth, at least on the surface.

For once Best was uncertain how to proceed. How to go about finding out whether their daughter was still alive and well or whether they had not seen her since 1866 after she had failed to turn up for a performance of *It's Never Too Late to Mend*.

Given their apparently robust character, he decided on a straightforward approach.

'It's about your daughter, Ida,' he said carefully.

He saw immediately that this was a mistake. The pair instantly became rigidly alert, shot glances at each other and looked at him expectantly.

'You've found her!' exclaimed Edie, reaching for her husband's hand.

They gazed at him wide-eyed with hope.

Best was caught off guard. He shook his head quickly. 'Er ... No. I'm sorry. I just wanted to ask you some questions about her. What happened ...' He was struggling. 'There's a case ...'

'That girl that was murdered at the Princess's,' said Rupert bluntly. 'You think the same thing happened to Ida.'

'No. No, I don't,' exclaimed Best. 'Well – ' he fell back – 'I just don't know. I'm looking at all the possibilities. Some

of them will have nothing to do with Esther Gibbons's death.'
He avoided their eyes. 'It's what we do,' he finished lamely.

They stared at him. Sixteen years and the pain was still raw.

'Why don't you,' he said, 'why don't you just tell me what happened?'

They did. It transpired that they had been touring in the North-west at the time, dashing from town to town, theatre to theatre. Sometimes letters caught up with them, sometimes not. Lives so rushed and busy that although they were aware that they hadn't heard from Ida for some time, they put it down to post going astray or Ida being as busy as they were.

Maybe she was playing one role in the evening then rehearsing another for the rest of the night – as was common practice.

Finally, her silence became overwhelming and when their own letters to her remained unanswered they wrote to the theatre manager to enquire whether their daughter might be ill. This was a big step to take. They might spoil Ida's chances by being a nuisance or making her appear to be a problem by suggesting that she suffered from ill health. Actors who proved to be a problem could lose work and actor-managers could successfully blacklist anyone who fell into that category. Indeed, they often tried to keep their illnesses a secret lest it get around that they were not available for employment.

The answer they received from the manager horrified them. Six weeks earlier Ida had failed to turn up for a performance and had not been seen since. They were appalled when told that no one had made a serious effort to find her, the supposition being that she had merely gone off on a whim.

'We told the police,' explained Edie, 'but they were not much interested in a missing actress. They took the same attitude as the manager and said that she was entitled to go off if she wanted. She was an adult. There was no law against it and nothing they could do about it.'

Tears were gathering in her eyes as she recollected the despair and frustration.

'But I knew a top man at Scotland Yard,' Rupert put in, 'and as a favour he got Detective Inspector Rogers to look into it. But he found nothing.'

144

Best's heart sank at the name. DI Rogers had died of the typhoid he had caught while on an extradition case in Naples.

Might he have made out a report? If so, would it still be around? It was so long ago. Even if it was, would he be able to find it among the chaos in their cramped offices, where old files, books and registers were piled up in disarray on the stairs.

Best explained none of this to the Blackmores, merely saying, 'I'll see if I can locate the file. Of course, this being an unofficial inquiry, you do appreciate that there might not be one?'

They nodded helplessly.

'I'll do what I can,' he said, 'then I'll come back to you. Meanwhile, if you would tell me all you can about Ida and give me the names of any of her friends.'

'Thank you,' said Rupert. 'We appreciate it.'

His wife nodded. They were pathetically grateful that at last someone might be taking their quest seriously.

Don't thank me yet, thought Best. He had a growing feeling that any news he brought them would be bad.

Twenty-Eight

After he had learned more about Ida Blackmore, Best began to compare her with Esther Gibbons. If they had shared a similar fate, might there not be similarities between the girls themselves? Things that had caused them either to be selected by the killer or to have fallen into his trap?

He still doubted that Ida really was another victim. The time gap was so wide and, after all, she could have gone off intentionally without telling her parents. People did that. All the time.

It was even possible that she had not liked them. She might

have blamed them for giving her such a hard life in the theatre as a child, a life from which escape seemed impossible. The boys, having been properly educated, could go into other professions but the girls knew nothing else.

When Best had seen Ida's performance, she had seemed happy enough but who could really tell?

Might she have seen the chance of doing something, something she liked better, and snatched it? Or had she run away with someone of whom her parents disapproved?

They swore there was no such person. But how were they to know when they were miles away, performing in Liverpool and Manchester?

Then, of course, there was the possibility that she had been pregnant and felt too ashamed to tell them. She might have thrown herself in the Thames – plenty of girls in that situation did so. If he could find the Rogers report he would discover whether the DI had checked if any likely bodies had resurfaced at the time.

Meanwhile, just in case Ida *had* been murdered and by the same person or persons as Esther, Best concentrated on any obvious similarities between the girls.

Their backgrounds seemed quite different. For a start, Ida was a stage child. Esther was not.

Esther lived at home with her parents in Somers Town and Ida, to Best's surprise, at Kean House in Montague Street. The very place where their first victim, Talisman, was living when he was murdered.

But, again, she had been there so long ago this probably did not signify. It could be just one of those awful coincidences.

But why hadn't the landlady, Mrs Hodgson, mentioned the girl when they were talking about incidents at the Princess's? He'd had the feeling she was holding something back.

He must go to see her again.

When it came to similarities, both girls were seventeen when they disappeared. Both had fair hair and skin and blue eyes. Esther had the intriguing combination of her father's chiselled features and her mother's waif-like fairness which apparently had helped her seem vulnerable one minute and quite strong the next. By all accounts it was this fascinating mixture that had contributed to her success as Shakespeare Jarvis.

From what Best remembered about Ida she was a much more sturdy girl than Esther. But, then, he reminded himself, he had only seen her dressed as a boy criminal and in a very masculine setting, that of a male prison.

He cogitated a little more. Two definite similarities: they both had just been given great acting opportunities and were succeeding with them, and both had been playing boys. They were on the threshold of life and, maybe, greatness, because both had been the type of performers who drew your eye and held it. They were also good actresses.

Several differences, many similarities. For any more comparisons he must find DI Rogers's file on Ida, if there was one, and send Smith off to speak to her friends.

Detective Chief Superintendent Williamson put his head around the door.

'We've got permission for you to issue reward posters asking for information about the murders and the apprehension of Jerry Banks,' he said.

'I've not got that much on him yet,' said Best.

'Maybe not. But he was her boyfriend, or thought he was. He was heard rowing with her and then ran off. Suspicious enough, I'd say, and we've got a warrant. We must find him. Also,' he added pragmatically, 'it might make people realize that we *are* trying to solve these cases. Don't want to make it look as if we've nearly let the murderer slip through our fingers again.'

Best didn't blame Williamson for being so sensitive about that. The department was already under attack over the robbery and murder of Mr Isaac Frederick Gold in a carriage of the London to Brighton Railway. A railway guard had immediately delivered a suspect into police hands – one Percy Lefroy – but that was before a body had been found.

Lefroy had explained the blood on his clothes and his dishevelled appearance on arrival at Preston Park Railway Station by claiming that *he* had been attacked as the train was passing through the Merstham Tunnel.

The suspicious guard spotted a chain hanging from Lefroy's sock and, on pulling on it, found a watch attached. The injured man claimed it was his and that he had hidden it to prevent it being stolen.

A Detective Sergeant Holmes took a statement from Lefroy, then escorted him to hospital, where his wounds were found to be minor.

En route to Lefroy's home the DS learned that a body had been found at the trackside by the Balcombe Tunnel, fifteen miles beyond Merstham.

There had been no watch on the body and Holmes was told to ask Lefroy the make and number of the one he claimed was his. He instantly came up with the number but could not remember the name of the maker. Since Holmes had no idea of the make of his own watch he gave Lefroy the benefit of the doubt.

When he arrived back at the police station another telegram was waiting. This one instructed him to detain Lefroy. But it was too late. The bird had flown.

This incident was seized upon with delight by the Press despite the fact that Holmes was a railway policeman. They loved to attack Howard Vincent and his new CID, which *Punch* had christened 'The Defective Department'.

When the CID *did* take over the Lefroy case the *Daily Telegraph* published Vincent's plea for assistance in tracing Lefroy (whose real name was Mapleton) and printed the sparse official description. However, they augmented this, 'in the interest of justice', with a much more detailed one they had compiled themselves. For good measure they added a sketch of the suspect 'by a gentleman who knew Lefroy and had frequent opportunities of noting his characteristics'.

To their credit the Yard had the sketch copied and distributed. Finally, after several erroneous arrests, and with the aid of 'information received', they nabbed Lefroy.

They found he had cut off his whiskers and moustache but, to the further delight of the Press, was in possession of a false set.

Punch then published a cartoon of Vincent reading a detective story surrounded by fictional detective paraphernalia, false moustaches, handcuffs, a dark lantern and a carnival mask. The caption declared that Vincent might be 'Directeur des Affaires Criminelles de la Police Metropolitan de Londres' and a 'Membre de la Faculté de Droit et de la Société Generales des Prisons de Paris' and yet 'when there's practical detecting to be done, to be done, this Director's lot is not a happy one.'

The refrain was of course a parody of the police sergeant's song from the Gilbert and Sullivan Comic Opera *The Pirates of Penzance*. The French allusions were a reference to Vincent's study of the methods of the Parisian Sûreté, which had won him charge of the Scotland Yard detectives.

Small wonder Vincent, Williamson and the Commissioner wanted to show they were taking prompt action regarding the two murders at the Princess's Theatre.

Best chose to keep to himself the fact that there might, in fact, be three murders. No point in starting a panic. They'd learn soon enough if that were so.

'How much reward?' he asked instead.

'A hundred pounds for information about the killer of Miss Gibbons and fifty pounds for the capture of Banks. Then a hundred pounds for Talisman's murderer.'

'You want them separate?'

'Have to, I think.'

When Williamson had gone, Best got down to composing the reward posters beginning with '£100 REWARD' to be printed very large and bold and, underneath it, the word 'MURDER' to be printed even larger and bolder. Then he continued in the usual manner, giving the day, date, time and place of the murder and the name of the victim. He was about to continue with the means of murder when he stopped.

No, he wouldn't mention how she died. It was the usual practice but he'd always thought it a bit stupid to let out so much information as well as to inflame further all those compulsive letter writers out there who would send in silly advice, mostly useless information, and false confessions.

Occasionally, the letters produced a glint of gold in the form of useful information but usually not enough to justify the time wasted on them.

He went on: 'The above reward will be paid by Her Majesty's Government to any person who shall give information as shall lead to apprehension and conviction of the guilty person or persons.'

Then came the part that offered a pardon to any accomplice who didn't actually do the deed but who was prepared to come forward and inform on his accomplice.

Under the '£50 REWARD' to be printed large and bold but not quite so large and bold as the '£100 REWARD', he requested information regarding the whereabouts of Jerry Banks, for whom a warrant had been issued on suspicion of murdering Miss Gibbons.

Then he wrote out Jerry's description.

Best turned to the scrap of paper inscribed with Smith's schoolboy script. He hoped John George had gathered sufficient details to stop the *Daily Telegraph* from making them look like fools again.

Fortunately he had gleaned a great deal. Jerry, it seemed, was five feet nine inches tall, was slim, had a veritable bush of auburn hair, a chipped front tooth and the habit of scratching his head and pulling his right ear lobe when puzzled. He also had a slightly rolling gait. Thank goodness Smith had included the gait. Cheadle was very keen on descriptions of how a suspect walked.

Best finished the notice off with details of where the information should be sent, added the Commissioner's name, to be printed quite large and bold, and the date.

He sighed and drew over another sheet of paper and set to work on a notice about Talisman's murder.

After that, maybe he'd be allowed to get on with what he had been about to do, reading Detective Inspector Rogers's report on his search for Ida Blackmore.

Twenty-Nine

So, she thought she was clever evading him like that. Spoiling his plans, being devious, as all women were, even when pretending to be men. Thinking she could claim all the privileges of both sexes but the responsibilities of neither.

Well, she was wrong.

He could wait.

He'd always been good at that. He had patience. He'd had to have with a mother like his. One who led them all a dance. Doing what she wanted. Thinking him stupid.

But he had surprised her with his planning and patience and his learning by observation. He'd had plenty of time for that when he was hanging about waiting for her. She had been surprised when she discovered that he was clever with his hands, could make things, even invent things.

She had been even more surprised when he made her money disappear right before her eyes just like he'd seen that magician do. And that she wasn't able to tell what he was thinking or going to do next. While waiting and watching all that time he had learned to act. That had surprised her a lot.

At last, Best was able to do what he had set out to do. Settle down to read Rogers's report.

As he expected, the DI had concentrated on talking to people at the theatre and at Kean House.

Rogers had first spoken to the actor-manager, George Vining, who held total control of the Princess's Theatre from 1863 to 1869. He had had a leading role as a prisoner alongside Ida Blackmore when she was playing Joseph, the boy prisoner, in *It's Never Too late to Mend* and was the man who stepped forward to calm the audience when Joseph was whipped.

One item which immediately caught Best's eye was Vining's address. He lived in *Upper* Montague Street. Kean House was in Montague Street, which raised doubts about the actor-manager's claims that he knew very little about Ida other than professionally.

Surely they must have bumped into one another en route to the theatre or in the neighbourhood? Then again, maybe not. Vining would probably have taken a cab to the theatre.

Best had noticed how Barrett and other leading actors arrived wearing lustrous boots – a sure sign they didn't walk through the filthy London streets as would the likes of Ida. And, of course, Ida might be only one of several of the cast who lived in that part of Bloomsbury.

Her fellow actors and supers were little help with information about reasons for Ida's disappearance. They had not noticed any change in her manner apart from natural excitement at being given a chance to shine at last. Neither had they seen any evidence of a passionate liaison nor heard any complaints about unwelcome advances.

Would they have told Rogers if it involved someone with control over their prospects? Someone like an actor-manager? Probably not. Best had noticed such reticence when questioning the servants of wealthy men.

But time sometimes blew away such restraints. He might find out more from them now. With luck, some of them would still be working at the Princess's.

One name on Rogers's list caught Best's eye: Alexander Pearman, aged fifty-two, who had a utility role as another of the prisoners. But Best was unable to recall the reason why the name chimed with him.

He worried at it for a few minutes, then let it go. It would come to him later. Elusive memories usually did, he found. But only after he had set the search in motion by applying some intense thought to the matter first.

Mrs Hodgson, the Kean House landlady, had admitted herself as puzzled as everyone else by her lodger's sudden departure. Ida had gone to the theatre that evening as usual although on this occasion she had left Kean House early. About two hours early. And she had seemed a little excited.

The landlady had not noticed signs of any special liaison, passionate or otherwise, and had added that Ida appeared to be quite a proper young lady. Not loose in her morals like some young actresses nor any trouble as a guest.

Of course, thought Best, Mrs Hodgson would not wish her lodging house to get a bad name. Attitudes among theatricals were somewhat more relaxed then, the theatre's climb to respectability having only just begun. Nonetheless, even then, actresses had had to guard their reputations.

Ida's parents had asked her friends if they knew anything, Rogers noted, but to no avail. Therefore the only thing left for him to do was to check whether any bodies answering Ida's description had been dragged out of the Thames or the Regent's Canal or found in dark alleys. Plenty had. But none were Ida.

That was not much help, thought Best as he reinserted the report pages in their folder.

So, back to the theatre to find out whether time had loosened any tongues.

Best turned right as he came out of Great Scotland Yard then left as he reached the south side of Trafalgar Square.

From Cockspur Street he turned right into the Haymarket, which was fairly quiet at the moment. It would soon come alive with the crowds going to the theatres, pubs and other houses of entertainment, cabbies touting for their custom and flower sellers and prostitutes offering their wares.

The fine rain, that had been throwing a veil of mist over the grey streets, had now eased off and a weak October sun filtered through the grey-brown clouds.

Best resisted the urge to jump into one of the cabs lined up in the centre of the road. The walk would freshen him up, get his mind working, as well as save some money, essential now he was becoming a family man. Even if the fare was approved, reimbursement from the Receiver took for ever.

It came to him just after he had walked around the western half of Regent's Circus South, or Piccadilly Circus as it was now starting to be called, and struck off up into Regent's Street.

Pearman was the name of the young ballet dancer who had died as the result of the fire at the Princess's in 1863. Sarah Pearman. That was it.

Was Alexander Pearman, the actor on Rogers's list, a relation of hers? Aged fifty-two. He could have been her father. Best stopped to cogitate on that possibility. But was it pertinent? Revenge as a motive?

Certainly George Vining had been criticized for the theatre's lack of adequate fire precautions. Subsequently, Best remembered, some people had been outraged by the spectacular fire scene in his next production, *The Streets of London*, which was staged only a few months after the tragedy. They felt that it was not only unfeeling but in very bad taste.

But Best could not imagine why a father would seek revenge by killing another actress. Not unless she had been involved with Vining or some other person of importance.

At Regent's Circus North, Best turned right into Oxford Street, girding his loins for another round of chats, this time trying to move witnesses back in time. Making the past come to life again.

At the theatre a telegram was awaited him. It contained the results of Esther's post-mortem. At last! She had died from the effects of a large dose of potassium cyanide.

Best groaned.

Not only were the cyanides among the deadliest of poisons and the quickest of killers but they were, like arsenic, one of the most readily available. Not only were they used in photography, the arts and science but also in food flavourings such as almond, peach or cherry essences.

They were even, for heaven's sake, constituents of easily obtained medicines such as laurel water and Scheele's Acid, a sedative and an indigestion formula which had killed quite a number of people by means of accidental overdose. Of course, such 'accidents' were not always what they appeared to be but it was often hard to prove otherwise.

No wonder a trial judge had remarked that secret poisoning was rife in London and Alfred Swaine Taylor, the noted toxicologist, held that many 'cholera deaths' were in fact due to poisoning.

Best was relieved about one thing. Esther must have died very quickly. Possibly within seconds. That might bring a little comfort to the parents and also to Smith, who had confessed his response to the mother's fears.

That was another habit of which he must rid Smith – confessing. He should learn from the criminals and crafty lawyers: only admit to facts against you which cannot be disproved and then give them an innocent explanation.

Of course Esther *could* have lived for up to an hour or more but not, Best would imagine, after such a large dose.

More interesting was the fact that there was no evidence of rape or other sexual interference. Quite strange that. Did it mean that the murder was nothing to do with sex? In a way he wished it had been. He could understand that. A rejected man acting in a sudden fury of resentment.

But, he reflected, someone acting in a sudden fury doesn't resort to poison. Not unless they have it to hand already.

Best tucked the telegram away in his overcoat pocket and began his quest to discover who had worked at the Princess's back in 1864.

Rosa's eyes were wide with delight.

'It's beautiful,' she said. 'Quite beautiful.'

She was in the Princess's Painting Room gazing at one of the backdrops for *The Romany Rye*. It was a gypsy encampment golden with autumn glory.

It was a long, high, slice of a room containing enormous stretching frames on which vast canvases were hung to be moved up and down by powerful windlasses. In the middle stood a long, rough table overflowing with sketches, model stages, brushes and jam pots of foul smelling paints. The smell made Rosa feel a little sick but she was so pleased to be there she managed to overcome this.

'And this one,' said Wilson Barrett, 'is Craigsnest Hall.'

'The home of the young master who one of the gypsy girls runs off with,' Rosa exclaimed. 'It's amazing!'

And it was. A picturesque old hall by a lake.

'Beverly's a genius,' Barrett admitted, smiling at her enthusiasm.

Rosa realized that scenic artists were very important to theatres like the Princess's and the Lyceum. In consequence, their names were given due prominence in the programmes alongside the titles of their scenes.

Beverly, whose full name was William Roxby Beverly, was the most famous and talented scenic artist of them all.

'We were lucky to get him,' ventured Rosa. She knew he often worked at Drury Lane.

'Absolutely,' agreed Barrett. He laughed. 'But he doesn't like the built stuff.'

Rosa smiled. She *thought* she knew what he meant and took a chance that she was right. 'So, no columns, porches or sticking out mantelpieces?'

'No,' Barrett agreed. 'He thinks the properly painted single surface is enough. No chicken wire and papier mâché for him!'

They both laughed companionably.

Barrett looked pleased that she understood but he had not yet offered her a part in *The Romany Rye*. He had told her that he would show her some of the scenery and tell her about the play to make up for the nasty trick played on her by some member of the cast. Perhaps, now they had got on so well, an offer would follow?

'It's going to be quite a production,' he enthused. 'Nearly forty characters, thirty-three of them of some significance. A host of auxiliaries, seventeen scenes, a dog and some live birds!'

'Seventeen scenes!'

Rosa clapped her hands with delight, her dark eyes shining. 'I can't wait to see it!'

'Neither can I,' said Barrett.

Watching in the shadows and staring at Rosa another man muttered, 'You will never see it!'

'We won't allow it, will we?' said another voice.

Thirty

'I've been thinking,' said Smith rather self-consciously. 'You know what I think? I think it's something to do with these breeches parts the girls were playing.'

Best considered this notion for a moment or two. He had been urging the young man to apply his mind to the evidence so he ought not to discourage him when he did, even though he was talking nonsense.

'What makes you think that?'

'Well . . .' Smith hesitated, endeavouring to marshal his thoughts. 'Well,' he said again, 'look at it like this. Firstly –' he pulled at his little finger – 'firstly, the two women had been playing them sort of parts, pretending they were lads.' He took a deep breath. 'An' I know we don't know whether Ida is dead but . . .'

'She could well be,' said Best.

'Right,' said Smith. 'So, secondly – ' he moved to the next finger – 'we know that some people don't like women doing that. Some even think it's disgusting.'

Best nodded encouragingly. He hoped this wasn't going to take too long. He was beginning to wish he hadn't started Smith off on all this. He was fine as he was. A sharp, hard-working, keen copper.

'Then – ' the middle finger came into play. 'Then, there's this business of her wearing a boy's cap when she was found – and having a cigar stuck in her mouth in that terrible way.'

'It's certainly a possibility,' said Best. 'One of several of course.' He paused. 'But how would Talisman fit into this?'

'Well,' said Smith uncertainly, wagging his index finger up and down. 'Either he doesn't – his murder has nothing to do

157

with the others. Or, Talisman found out what the murderer was up to and he was silenced by him.'

'Don't forget that he was murdered *before* Esther.'

Smith looked down uncertainly at his fingers. 'But he might, somehow, have known what the murderer planned,' he finished lamely and blushed. 'Or – or perhaps seen him getting familiar with her.'

'Possibility,' said Best. 'Good bit of deduction. And Jerry Banks?'

'He had nothing to do with it.'

Best nodded again.

The idea of revenge by the burns victim's relative was beginning to grow on him and push out everything else.

'What would be the point of these murders?' he asked.

'Well . . .' Smith floundered. 'You know. He's just off his head and wants to punish these girls. Teach them a lesson.'

'Not much point in teaching someone a lesson if you kill them,' laughed Best. 'They can't exactly put it into practice, can they?!'

Smith reddened again and Best wished he had held his tongue.

'No,' he insisted, 'but it might warn off other women from doing it . . .'

'But how could it if they don't know *why* the murders were committed?'

That had Smith stumped for a moment. Then, struggling, he said, 'No, but they might begin to realize – he's left us messages in a way – and especially if he did some more then they'd know.'

Best shuddered. 'God, that's a terrible thought!'

He paused to indicate that he was giving the matter proper weight. 'It's certainly an idea to think about.'

He could tell that Smith was disappointed. The lad knew him too well. 'Why don't you follow it up? Try to find out who might feel that way about breeches roles – without arousing their suspicions of course. Meanwhile, go over to the Yard and get the full post-mortem report, please.'

It transpired that Alexander Pearman was still playing utility parts and acting as a super at the Princess's and he turned out to be not at all what Best had expected.

There was no sign of a grieving parent here but, Best reminded himself, it was all a long time ago.

Alex Pearman was a scrawny, scraggy little man with a bulbous forehead and blackened stumps for teeth. He must be close to seventy, Best thought, and mystified as to why a policeman would want to speak to him about something which happened all those years ago.

'What's there to tell about it?' he muttered sulkily. 'It was in all the papers.'

'Must have been terrible for you,' said Best.

'Aye. She was my daughter after all. Worse for her though.'

Well, that was obvious.

'They'd been told though, you know.'

Best frowned.

'Who had?'

'The girls, the dancers.'

'Told what?'

'To be careful, course. Not to get too near the gas flames. Some of them took no notice!' he said with a note of indignation in his voice. 'Had to be fined, some of them, and they still did it!'

'Yes, but shouldn't there have been proper guards around the gas flames?'

'Oh, aye, I suppose. But there were no regulations about it then you know.'

Best was mystified as to why this man was defending the people whose carelessness had cost his daughter her life.

'But surely common sense would tell the managers to take proper precautions?'

Pearman shrugged petulantly.

'Mebbe. Some did an' the Princess's was no worse than t'others – better than some.' He sniffed. 'Anyway, when they did give the girls some of that stuff to soak their petticoats in a lot of them said they hadn't time and it didn't last anyway.'

'But the managers refused to fireproof the top layer, the costume,' said Best, 'claimed it would ruin the material.' He had been doing his homework. 'So there wasn't much point

159

in the girls' doing the petticoats, was there?'

'Dunno about that,' Pearman said, 'but like they said, there was a lot more women's dresses caught fire outside the theatre in their own homes – specially with those crinolines.'

He glanced around furtively to check whether anyone else was listening to this conversation and Best realized why he was so stoutly defending the management. Of course. I *am* getting slow, he thought.

Ever since his daughter's death they had looked after Pearman. Kept him in work despite his ageing and declining appearance. They were under no obligation to do so.

It wasn't until the following year, after another ballet girl death, that the Lord Chamberlain's recommendations became regulations to be posted up in every theatre. Then came the suggestion that the manager should be fined for allowing unguarded gaslights and charged with manslaughter in cases where neglect could be proved following a burns death.

That had got them sitting up a bit. But the suggestion of regular police inspections, such as they had in Paris, was rejected because, as was pointed out in a letter to *The Times*, 'inspection has never been a popular remedy even for admitted evils in England'.

Best realized there was not much point in continuing this conversation with a man so determined to defend the management.

'Anyway,' he said finally, 'I'm sorry about your daughter.'

Pearman shrugged and looked down, muttering something Best could not catch. Then his head shot up. 'What's all this about, anyway? Resurrecting all this old stuff?'

He could have chosen a better word, thought Best.

Best shrugged as well. 'Oh, the police like to keep abreast of these things and I'm just interested in everything that has happened in this theatre.'

'You'll be here for ever then,' said Pearman ungraciously.

Best felt that could be true.

Thirty-One

'I agree with John George,' said Helen. 'It's something to do with those breeches roles.'

Best looked at her disbelievingly.

'Why?'

'For the reasons he gave, of course.'

Best shook his head. 'I can't see it.'

'That's because you're not looking.' She handed him another wet paintbrush. 'But your burned ballet dancer theory has now gone and—'

'No it hasn't,' Best interrupted.

Helen frowned. 'But you said he didn't care. The father didn't blame the theatre.'

'He *said*.'

'You don't believe him?'

'I think he might just be saying that to keep the steady work he gets despite his age and unappealing aspect and to throw us off his scent.'

'Which it hasn't done?'

'No.'

Helen sighed.

'I have a lot more experience of people telling lies than you, my dearest,' he reminded her as he patted the brushes dry. 'All coppers have. When I first joined the force I couldn't believe what good liars so many people were. Second nature to them it was. They tripped me up a few times, I can tell you.'

'I appreciate that,' she said as she dried her hands and took the brushes from him, 'but even if you *are* right that doesn't mean you should just dismiss John George's idea out of hand.'

'I didn't.'

'But you don't think it's very likely?'

'No.'

'Why?'

'Well, so many actresses start out playing boys, Ellen Terry, for instance and even the now ultra respectable Mrs Bancroft when she was Marie Wilton. She played dozens.'

'Ah, yes. But she was in burlesque.'

'I can't see what difference that makes.'

'Well, it does.'

'And look at those male impersonators in music hall. I haven't heard of the Great Little Tilley being attacked.'

'Well, going by the current experience you'd only hear about it when she was dead. In any case – ' she took off her smock and led him over to the couch – 'those male impersonators in music hall don't even pretend to look like men. They wear corseted tops and tights with a fringe around the top of their legs. The only male things about them are their hats and canes. The whole thing is just an excuse to show off their legs.'

'Exactly. And what could be more provocative than that?'

'Not in the way I mean. These music hall women are not really trying to look like men. It's a joke that the audience shares. But in the theatre it's taken much more seriously and they do wear male clothing.'

He helped her sit down before she continued with a smile: 'You must remember, dear, that I have more experience of male attitudes towards women whom they think are being too daring and independent. They hate it. Really *hate* it. You can see it in their eyes and hear it in the vicious things they say.'

'What about the little boys who play girls or the men who play old ladies?'

'Not the same.'

He waited for her to explain, as he knew she would.

'When girls are pretending to be men they appear to be assuming all the privileges of that sex. The freedom, the power. The reverse *can't* be true because women have neither. There are *no* privileges.'

Oh, we were on to that subject. He could point out that

162

many women had the advantage of doing nothing all day while the men had the pleasure of working hard to keep them. But he didn't.

'Don't look like that, Ernest,' she said. 'I'm serious. I think you're missing something here.'

'And I think that just because you have a soft spot for John George you are taking his side.'

'I hope you were encouraging when he suggested this?'

He nodded but couldn't keep the guilt out of his eyes.

'Fairly,' he admitted.

She shook her head. 'Tch. Tch. You don't deserve such loyalty, Ernest Best.' She reached out her hand and touched his cheek. 'But you are an uncommonly handsome fellow. A bit flash of course.'

He hoped their steamy kisses and passionate embraces would divert her away from the subject. On another occasion they had made love on this couch as soon as he got home. But that wasn't too practical an idea at the moment.

When they paused for breath she returned to the subject.

He defended his position by referring to Charles Dickens's response to seeing Marie Wilton as Pippo in *The Maid and the Magpie.*

'He didn't find it offensive.'

She made a face at him to show that she knew he was being provocative. Helen thought Dickens's heroines were pathetic creatures. Even Best had to admit that, unlike Helen, they would not have been among the first to have become members of the London Women's Suffrage Society.

'Such a hypocrite.' She struggled to her feet. 'I'll read you what he *really* said about it.'

'No need . . .'

But she was already searching through the bookcase by the wall that served her with reading matter when she rested from her painting.

'Here we are. Mr Forster's *Life* of the gentleman in question.'

Best crossed his eyes at her but when she had found the page she read it out:

'I went to the Strand Theatre, having taken a stall before-hand, for it is always crammed. I really wish you would go to see *The Maid and the Magpie* burlesque there. There is the strangest thing in it that I have ever seen on the stage – the boy Pippo, by Miss Wilton. While it is astonishingly impudent (must be, or it couldn't be done at all), it is so stupendously like a boy, and unlike a woman, that it is perfectly free from offence. I have never seen such a thing. She does an imitation of the dancing of the Christy Minstrels – wonderfully clever – which, in the audacity of its thorough-going, is surprising. A thing you *cannot* imagine a woman's doing at all; and yet the manner, the appearance, the levity, impulse, and the spirits of it are so exactly like a boy, that you cannot think of anything like her sex in association with it.'

'How typical, claiming spirit and impulsiveness as male only traits.'

'Sounds fine to me,' said Best, dodging his head about as she threatened to aim the book at him.

'But seriously,' she said.

He groaned.

'Seriously, it's much worse now with all this creeping respectability on the stage. Those actresses afraid to do certain Shakespeare roles and even that Irving giving mealy-mouthed lectures about playing Rosalind or Imogen, saying how pure they were really and how it was all right if done in modest taste but that the faintest hint of indecorous dressing was fatal.' She paused. 'In any case, does that man ever stage *As You Like It* or *Cymbeline*?'

'Er . . .' Best shook his head. 'No.'

'And all those male critics saying women were fine playing men as long as you could still tell they were womanly and that their comic sides were not given too much rein!'

Best crossed his eyes at her again and she giggled.

'I'm preaching.'

'Just a little.'

She rang the bell for Jessie. 'Let's get you something to drink.'

It was their custom after such little spats each to offer the other some olive branch. She'd apologized for her preaching, so he said, 'All right. I will treat the idea more seriously. But, to be honest, I'm not quite sure what I can do about it.'

'You can make sure that that girl Rosa is safe.'

Thirty-Two

After he received the message Best left the theatre by way of the stage door that led out into Castle Street East.

Omnibuses didn't go the exact route he wanted and in any case they took so long with all that stopping and starting to pick up the passengers strung out by the roadside.

He turned left and continued along the north side of Market Place. In passing, he offered a small lament for the loss of the lively Oxford Market, the large arcaded building which until last year had stood in the centre of this space, its high turret visible over the surrounding rooftops.

As he turned right into Great Portland Street the light was starting to fade and the air grow cooler. If he walked briskly he should warm up.

The street lights came on one by one. At first their smoky yellow glow seemed unnecessary but as Best progressed north towards Devonshire Street they became beacons in the descending gloom.

By the time he crossed Marylebone High Street his exertions had indeed caused a warm glow to spread through Best but it did little to lift his spirits. His was such a sad errand.

He turned left into Nottingham Street and there it was before him next to the old burial grounds: St Marylebone Workhouse.

It was a vast establishment – one of London's busiest work-houses, sheltering around two thousand souls. There were casual blocks for those staying only one night, wards for the aged and infirm, dormitories for the able-bodied, workrooms, schoolrooms, chapels, administration offices, an enormous dining hall, a board room and a mortuary. Indeed, to help take the strain, a second building had just been erected in Ladbroke Grove.

It was also a place of some notoriety and fame. The notoriety began when a master and his staff were accused of whipping young female inmates. Rehabilitation came later when another master and his wife, out walking in nearby Regent's Park, helped rescue the two hundred skaters who fell into the freezing water of the boating lake after the ice broke. They took the survivors back to the workhouse where they were looked after – and forty bodies to its mortuary.

The workhouse had gained further fame when Charles Dickens wrote about his role on one of its inquest juries. He had found St Marylebone Workhouse better than most of its kind.

The place was also familiar to Best. He had gone there to inspect the bodies of the canal boatmen killed in the Regent's Park Explosion of 1874. He recalled standing on its steps watching the crowds hurrying up to Madame Tussaud's Waxworks in the Marylebone Road, where, it was claimed, they captured murderers 'to the life'.

If only it were that simple, he thought as he made his way around the back to the mortuary.

The body lay on a marble slab in the crypt-like basement. At least it isn't hot this time, thought Best, although this body must have been in water longer than the canal boatmen. Consequently the smell of putrefaction was awful.

'He's been identified, sir,' said a young constable who had been waiting for him, 'by the van man.'

Best wondered how the van man had been able to swear that this wrinkled corpse, with flesh sloughing off its head and hands, was that of Jerry Banks, the strong young lad who used to hang from the rear of his express parcel vehicle, leaping off to make a delivery whenever the van stopped.

'We could tell by his uniform, to start with,' said the young policeman. 'And the scar on his right hand.' He pointed to a segment of skin hanging on to the lad's right thumb. 'An' of course there was his height and colouring. All like it said on the poster.'

So Smith had got it right. That was something.

'Then there were the things in his pockets.'

'Where was he found?'

'Just past the fist end,' put in George Harper, the Park Superintendent's Assistant, who was keeping a watching brief.

'The where?'

'Oh, that's what we call it.' He grinned apologetically and said, 'The eastern end of the boating lake by the archery grounds.'

Best knew Regent's Park's strangely shaped boating lake very well. From its wide central section which held two wooded islands that allowed the amateur boaters the opportunity to navigate around them in seamanlike fashion, to the three narrow, straggling octopus-like arms which led away from it.

Two of these arms formed a semicircle that appeared to be holding the sphere of the Royal Botanical Garden. The longest of these arms scooped southwards in a wide loop, trailing off into a fist-like shape which held a tiny island in its grasp. Then it undulated away under York Bridge to taper out just below the Archer's Lodge in the grounds of the Toxophilite Society.

Helen often went to the park to draw flowers, ducks and people. And, like so many Londoners, they had spent many a happy hour circumnavigating the islands or just sitting back contemplating the park's beautiful scenery.

Naturally, during the week and at this time of year there were fewer boaters and amblers along the footpaths and over the bridge. Otherwise, the lad's body might have been discovered sooner.

'It was a couple of the archery gentlemen what found him,' said Harper. 'They took a stroll down to the lake and saw something caught up by some reeds and branches, so they called the Park Superintendent – his house is close by.'

Best wondered idly why gentlemen strolled while the rest of humanity walked with the exception, of course, of the likes of Mr G. R. Sims, who pedestrianized.

Jerry Banks did what I've just done, thought Best. Walked, or ran, straight up here from Oxford Street. But he came that little bit farther – into Regent's Park. All that way and he did not change his mind. Such despair. How could someone forfeit their life so easily?

Then he recalled that he had just been about to do the same in Newcastle when he thought he had lost Helen.

Of course the lad might *not* have thrown himself into the water in despair at the news of Esther's death. What if he *had* gone to the Princess's Theatre that day, wanting to know what had happened, trying to see her body? He could have bumped into someone who wanted to silence him.

Now why would anyone want to do that?

Because he knew something? Had Esther told him about someone who had been 'bothering' her or a fear that she had?

'He wasn't tied up, weighted down or anything?' Best asked.

Harper shook his head. 'No sign of anything like that.'

'We'll have to treat it as suspicious nonetheless,' Best said.

Harper looked unhappy at this. The Park Superintendent would not be pleased.

As well as man hours lost to attendance at the inquest there might be other court appearances later and these could bring bad publicity in their wake. The coroner might enquire just why the body had remained undiscovered until a couple of strolling toxicologists took a break from exercising their pectoral muscles.

Best wasn't happy either. Another suspicious death to worry about. Another possible murder. Unlikely, perhaps, but he had to be sure.

He decided that rather than go on speculating and worrying he would just wait to hear what the post-mortem results had to say.

I want to make it last longer this time,' he said. 'Make her suffer.'

'You mustn't start getting careless.'

'How can you say that! I never am!'

'Oh, yes you are. Look at that business with the Painting Room.'

He was indignant. 'It all worked perfectly well until the last part.'

'That's the part that counts, isn't it? Punishing them.'

'It wasn't *my* fault that the stupid girl couldn't find her way to the Painting Room.'

'You should have taken that into consideration. That's all I'm saying. You should have remembered she was new. You're lucky the police didn't find out.'

'You're sounding more and more like my mother – an' I don't like that! You're all talk but no help when it comes down to it.'

'I keep a rein on you. Stop you from making terrible mistakes. Rushing straight in. I make you think it out.'

'It'll be all right this time.'

'It better be.'

He laughed. 'She won't be able to escape what I have planned – and she *will* suffer. I'll teach her to prance around like that!'

'That's good. Just keep your head.'

'Even that vile mother of mine would be proud of me and my plan.'

Thirty-Three

S mith was endeavouring to ingratiate himself with the cast and workers at the Princess's Theatre. While doing so, he was hoping to come upon a person who felt so strongly about breeches roles as to want to kill the actresses who performed them.

He suspected that Best was indulging him by giving him this task when in reality he thought it a daft idea. Turning it over in his mind now, it did begin to seem rather silly to him as well. Much too flimsy a reason to commit murder. Nonetheless, he'd been given the task, so he took a deep breath and got on with it.

He knew that he could scarcely ask the question outright: 'Does the idea of a girl playing male roles and dressing like a man enrage you?'

He must think ahead and devise a way to ease into the subject. A good plan, he decided, was to pretend that he had a young sister who wanted to become an actress. Then he could ask their advice as to how she should go about this.

This was another Best ploy: when you're stuck, ask people's advice. 'They love giving it,' Best insisted, 'but you won't have to mind looking ignorant or foolish.'

Lest someone expect this fictitious sister to materialize and also to counter any invitations that might come her way, he would explain that she was in service in Essex. That her mistress refused to give her more than her one half day off a week and on that she had to go to see their ailing mother.

Despite feeling a little guilty about this last lie, Smith felt quite proud of the ingenuity of his yarn. Particularly the fact that he had thought ahead to the possibility of being asked awkward questions.

It occurred to him that some people might wonder why he was wasting so much valuable police time on personal matters – so he interwove his actress questions with others pertaining to Talisman and Esther. He also made it clear that all the information gained would be useful in building up 'a picture of theatrical life'.

He'd discovered that it wasn't only Cheadle who talked all the time of 'pictures'. The theatricals were also keen on them but to them they were the scenes that met the eyes of the audience when the curtains were drawn back. Apparently, much effort was put into attempts to astound with these 'pictures'.

Should anyone point out that Best had already done that, built up a picture, he would say that his inspector had asked him to bring a fresh eye to the subject. Being artistic they would understand that.

It helped that the manly, open-faced young sergeant began

his quest by talking to the young actresses and female supers. This was not because he imagined himself irresistible to them but because they were the ones who might have experienced such anti-breeches attitudes or heard of them through gossip.

Best always said that if you were on the lookout for a predatory man you should ask the ladies which of their male acquaintances was prone to undue familiarity. Most men were unaware of such habits among their sex and even if they were either applauded them or saw them as only 'harmless fun'.

Smith soon found himself inundated with kindly advice to pass on to his sister. To his surprise he discovered that there was much more to the acting profession than merely pretending to be someone else.

The women informed him that there were no acting schools like they had in France and Germany, so his sister should try to get some experience in parish plays or to be taken on as a super at her local theatre. They would probably want her to supply her own costumes and pay her almost nothing. In fact, she might have to pay *them* for the privilege. Despite all this she was never to show signs of desperation. Managers hated that.

At the same time she should save up her pennies to take voice production lessons so that she might be heard from the stalls to the gods and elocution lessons so that, once heard, the voice did not jar. Singing and dancing instruction was also useful and private tuition in the art of acting from an established actor could be vital.

On her own, she should practise in front of a mirror how to walk on stage (heavier and firmer in tragedy for example) and how to stand.

Smith found their advice on the latter rather bewildering. For instance, they informed him, when standing sideways on stage the leg nearest the audience should never be held forward obscuring the back leg. Always, the far leg should be held forward. All very strange.

Naturally, as the conversations developed, they broached the kind of roles newcomers could expect to play and the actresses' experiences in playing them. Naturally, these included breeches roles. However, to his disappointment, from all this plethora of knowledge he gleaned little information regarding a possible suspect – so he changed tack.

He started asking about backstage gossip and jealousies but the actors and actresses became wary at this, sensing it might lead in the direction of a motive for murder.

So he changed tack again concentrating this time on the minor irritations of theatre work generally. Things like upstaging and refusing to look at the actor when he was speaking his lines – which tended to negate their power.

It appeared that these *could* become major irritations – as could the various methods of stealing work from under a colleague's nose.

'You sound just like us,' laughed Smith. 'You wouldn't believe the way detectives can sneak in and steal credit from someone else. They get up to all sorts of tricks.'

'Oh, I know what you mean,' exclaimed Mary Eastlake, happy that someone was treating her with respect and not hinting that she only got the lead roles due to her beauty and her rumoured relationship with Wilson Barrett. 'Look at that nasty prank they played on Rosa with that letter!'

Smith was instantly alert but he merely shrugged nonchalantly, smiled and shook his head.

'What was that?'

Mary Eastlake explained.

Which is how Detective Sergeant Second Class John George Smith became the first police officer to hear about the attempt to lure Rosa de la Drake – who just happened to be playing a breeches role – to a deserted painting room at midnight.

An attempt that had been taken to be merely a dirty trick played by jealous rivals. Which was the reason the incident had not been reported to any one of the many Scotland Yard detectives who had been in the theatre for days.

Thirty-Four

S mith felt that he must give Best this information as soon as possible but he wasn't sure where he was. He knew he had gone to St Marylebone Workhouse to view the body of Jerry Banks but had he gone home afterwards? Or on somewhere else? To see Jerry Banks's parents, perhaps?

Should he dash up to the workhouse in case Best was still there? If he wasn't, should he follow him to his home in Notting Hill? But if he did that, he left Rosa unaware and undefended again. He felt sure now that his idea was correct and that Rosa was in danger.

There was only one thing for it. He would send a telegram to the Yard, then wait for Rosa's arrival for the evening's performance and warn her. In the meantime, he would go to see Barrett and find out just why this information had been kept from them.

He marched up to the man's private sitting room at the far end of the west wing on the dress-circle floor, knocked loudly on the door, then entered before even waiting for an answer.

The startled actor-manager was lying back resting on a couch by his desk, play script in hand. He looked up indignantly. 'What the—?'

'Why,' asked Smith without preamble, 'did you not inform us about Rosa and the letter?'

Barrett looked at him coldly. He placed the play script on a side table, smoothed down his hair, and said stiffly, 'It was an internal matter.'

'I don't think so!' shouted Smith loudly and sharply enough to persuade the man that boyish looks did not indicate lack of purpose or authority. 'This girl could be in mortal danger.'

Barrett smiled indulgently. 'Oh, I don't think so, Sergeant. It

173

was just some theatre mischief. You must understand,' he said, sitting up and lowering his feet on to the floor, 'that the theatre is a closed world where rivalries and jealousies fester and—'

'And *you* must understand,' exclaimed Smith, thumping the mahogany desk which lay between them, 'that this is a serious matter. For God's sake, man, how many murders does it take to make you realize?!'

Barrett was taken aback. He wasn't used to his authority being questioned and was unsure how to react. He stood up, straightened his clothes and began to say something. Then he stopped. Smith knew that the seriousness of the matter was at last coming home to him.

They stared at each other for a moment, then Barrett indicated a seat beside the desk and took the one opposite.

Smith explained their theory as to the motive of the killer. That it was all about breeches roles. Esther Gibbons had been playing one of these when she died. Rosa was now doing so and she had received a letter designed to lure her to a deserted spot. It was only luck and her own ignorance which had saved her.

He refrained from mentioning the possibility that Ida Blackmore may also have been a victim. He saw by Barrett's expression he had made his point and that this was enough to be going on with.

'I did warn the women never to leave alone,' Barrett said defensively. 'You know they have their own corridor and stairs, which helps protect them. And I told Rosa not to take notice of any further notes from me unless they were signed in the particular way I showed her.'

Smith said nothing, just sighed and gazed wearily up into the corner of the room.

Leave silences, Best had told him. People need to fill them. But this one was not deliberate.

Eventually he spoke.

'Do you really think, Mr Barrett,' he said heavily, 'that this man will not find other ways to trap her?' He threw his arms wide and gazed about him. 'In this vast place the chances must be endless.'

There was another long pause and this time Barrett ended

it by nodding, chastened, and admitting, 'You're right, officer. What can we do?'

'I will see Rosa as soon as she comes in, warn her without frightening her too much, that she must not go *anywhere* alone or where she might be isolated.' He thought for a moment, then continued: 'I'll stay here, outside her dressing room.'

He stopped, waiting for objections about the privacy of the women's corridor but none came. 'I will keep an eye on her as she comes and goes. Then I'll escort her home.'

'Oh, I can get someone to do that,' said Barrett.

Smith raised his eyebrows. 'Someone you trust absolutely not to do her any harm?'

Barrett grimaced ruefully. 'No, I suppose not.'

Smith sat back.

Was that enough? Would Best have done more? If so, what?

He couldn't think of anything else, so, despite being tired and ravenously hungry, he went down to the stage door and sat there waiting for Rosa to arrive.

Barrett sent down a beef sandwich and a bottle of ale that helped Smith pass the waiting time and keep his strength up.

When Rosa did arrive she was clearly bemused by his news and all the attention but did not seem frightened.

That's because she doesn't believe it, thought Smith. I will have to persuade her to take care for my sake. Give her the idea that should I lose sight of her I would be in serious trouble. Which, in a way, isn't so far from the truth.

The young sergeant was not a naturally devious man but had begun to develop a certain cunning merely as a professional tool.

He was, of course, urged on in this by Best. To deceitfully engage a person's sympathy was, Best had informed him, just part of the job and for the greater good of all.

While waiting for the performance to begin, Smith sat quietly in the ladies' corridor outside Rosa's dressing room. His presence caused much giggling and several saucy asides, particularly from some young ladies who dashed out half dressed on their way to the lavatory or to an adjoining dressing room 'forgetting' that he was there.

175

Had they but known it, ladies' underwear was nothing new to Smith. He had spent many of his earlier years surrounded by such clothing which his widowed mother took in to wash.

Of course, as even he would admit, ladies' underwear with ladies inside it was a much more titillating prospect, but the responsibility that was weighing heavily upon him prevented his attention from wandering too much.

When Rosa eventually went down to the stage for her first appearance, Smith tagged along behind her. The other actors, presuming him to be besotted by the exotic Rosa, exchanged amused but puzzled glances. Why was Barrett allowing him such freedom?

Someone else noticed Smith's presence.

'So, they think they can outwit me, do they?' he muttered. 'I'll show them.'

'Don't get reckless. They must be suspicious. That's why he's here.'

'So, it's tonight then,' he said, taking a jemmy and a hammer from under a bench. 'They've forced my hand.'

'Don't be a fool. If you try to catch her now it will be noticed!'

'Oh, I won't try to catch her. She'll come to me. Just you watch!'

Rosa and Smith reached the wings in time for the end of Scene One, Act Three. The evil Clifford Armytage was coming offstage in company with Detective Cutts whom he had just informed of the probable whereabouts of the hero, Harold.

Rosa and Smith stood watching the frantic scene change as the outside of a London police station became the inside of the Jarvises' rooms in the Borough.

Once they were set up, Rosa took up her place on the sofa as the recuperating Shakespeare Jarvis while Bess, who had nursed him through a terrible fever, sat in an armchair by the fire, sewing and longing for the fugitive Harold.

An anxious Smith stood doggedly in the wings, never taking his eyes off Rosa. It had suddenly occurred to him that the murderer might *not* try to trap her offstage this time but, as with Talisman, to kill her onstage?

As that thought struck him, he wondered whether he ought to bring the whole performance to a halt. What would Best do? he thought desperately. He settled on never taking his eyes from her, constantly changing his position to keep her in view, no matter how much the stagehands cursed him when he got in their way.

He watched Shakespeare's reunion with his parents and the introduction of a 'Mr Smith', a mysterious man wearing a long green cloak and a slouch hat. This turned out to be none other than the fugitive, Harold, in disguise.

Harold had a passionate reunion with Bess from which the Jarvis family discreetly withdrew – through a doorway at the rear of the scenery – causing Smith almost to panic. He ran around the back to catch them emerging, ignoring the shouts of the stagehands. Then he ran back to the wings once again as they re-entered the scene.

When she exited at the other side of the stage to fetch food for the Jarvises' supper Smith was completely at a loss. Should he dash right around the back? Could he? Was it possible?

To his relief, Shakespeare soon returned with the supplies.

The family were then disturbed by the arrival of Detectives Cutts and Waters, armed with a search warrant. They arrested Mr Jarvis, mistaking him for Harold, and the curtain fell.

Rosa was not in the following scene, which took place at The Hawthorns, a richly furnished house in St John's Wood where the horrible Hetty is chiding Clifford for not yet making her an honest woman. She wants to show off her new-found wealth to her friends.

Rosa smiled and took pity on the anxious Smith.

'Come on,' she said. 'Let's go into the Green Room. I can tell by the music when I'm on again.'

The Green Room was only a couple of minutes from the stage. On the way Smith noticed that she was holding on to the right leg of her breeches. Once inside she revealed a long tear in the material.

'I never knew that the side of the table was so sharp. I tore it when I got up from the couch. Lucky I didn't cut myself.'

Rosa located a sewing pouch and a box of safety pins. There wasn't enough time for any sewing but, while Smith averted his eyes, she made an emergency repair with the safety pins.

Then they sat quietly side by side and relaxed a little.

It was warm in there and a great weariness began to steal over Smith. His eyes felt very heavy and it was only Rosa's lively chatter that kept them from closing completely.

'That's it,' said Rosa as the music swelled dramatically. 'We had better go now.'

Back in the wings Smith sat down just for a moment in one of the armchairs, which had been pushed offstage from the sitting room of The Hawthorns.

Although padded, it was a lady's armchair, smaller and more upright than the gent's lounging style and with very small arms to allow for the spread of a crinoline, all of which ensured that it was not really comfortable enough to encourage absolute relaxation. It was cramped, especially for such a big man.

So, in the now stifling heat, which had built up from the numerous gaslights and lime-lights, Smith resumed his vigil.

Rosa was on stage as Mr Jarvis was released in his own recognizance, the magistrate clearly only half believing that he had found the convict clothing he happened to be wearing when he was arrested and had been trying it on in readiness for a part in their new drama.

She came off again while Harold, the real escaped convict, and his wife Bess wandered the streets penniless before attempting to take shelter in a workhouse. This scene was recognized by the audience as a clever replication of the famous Luke Fildes heart-rending painting *Applicants for Admission to a Casual Ward* and was duly rewarded with much applause, which caused Smith to sit up, startled.

The fugitive couple did not go into the workhouse but took fright and wandered on.

More applause greeted 'The Slips' in Regent's Park, a canal basin where, under a bridge, Harold and Bess again seek shelter. Smith was very much looking forward to this scene having heard a great deal about it but he was struggling hard to keep his eyes open.

Over the bridge, taking the air on their way home, come

Clifford Armytage and Hetty, followed by her father, Seth Preene. Seth accosts Clifford, demanding that he marry Hetty or else he will tell the truth about the robbery of which Harold had been accused. A fight ensues during which Seth is pushed in the water. The sleeping Harold is awoken by his drowning shouts and jumps into the water to save him.

Neither Seth's shouts nor the audience's horrified response to his plight penetrated the mind of John George Smith, who, by now, despite the inadequacies of the lady's armchair, was fast asleep.

Rosa, who had taken another seat alongside him, saw no reason to wake him when she went back on stage again for the scene in the Borough Market at midnight and the action which would eventually lead to the dramatic finale.

She could come to no harm on stage surrounded by all those people and in front of an audience of two thousand.

Thirty-Five

R osa was already in trouble by the time the cast had all gathered at the Borough Police Station, where the recaptured Harold was put in the dock.

The tear in her breeches had lengthened so that it stretched right down the outside of her right thigh. There was imminent danger of it travelling further so that the side parted altogether.

To hide this fact she stood immobile, side-on to the audience with, as Smith might have noticed had he been awake, the wrong leg held forward and her right hand pulling the sides of the tear together.

After the final curtain calls she decided that she must do something about this and do it now, late as it was. She would go up to the wardrobe rooms and leave a note telling them she must have a new pair of breeches for tomorrow night.

But first, she would go to the Property Making Room near the stage door and speak to Mr Houghton about that table edge and the fact that the beer can she carried into the Borough Market was beginning to leak. That would give him plenty of time to put both things right before tomorrow night.

Although she realized that it was odd that she had never previously noticed that piece of metal jutting straight out from the table corner she put it down to those careless scene shifters the cast were always complaining about.

She needed to move quickly so as to catch Houghton, then dash up to the wardrobe rooms on the gallery floor and then get away home. She would manage all that better without her escort who still sat sleeping in a corner of the opposite wings.

It's not as if anyone has attempted to lure me anywhere, she reasoned, and I'm going to these places entirely of my own accord. In any case, the scene shifters would soon wake the sergeant and, she smiled indulgently, he would come rushing after her and they would all imagine it to be further proof of his passion for her.

As she made her way across the stage she stopped Harry Edgar, who, with the still young and new but much wiser Joe Burridge, was busy pushing the police station desk back towards the scene dock.

She pointed to Smith. 'When he wakes up tell him I've just dashed off up to wardrobe – ' she indicated her split side – 'and to Property. Then I'll be off home.'

Harry, who was a little deaf but didn't want his foreman to know in case it put his job in jeopardy, took the opportunity to wipe his brow and said, 'Righto, Miss.'

After she'd gone, he muttered to himself, *wardrobe then home*, then bent his back to his task again.

Rosa dodged around the rush of actors and supers hastily removing wigs and parts of their costumes as they walked and those stopping for a chat.

She hurried around Mr Barrett's dressing room, into the Royal Entrance, passed the Ladies Only stairs and the Green

Room and turned left into the passageway which ran along-side the supers' dressing room.

She had just reached the Property Making Room and lifted her right hand to knock on the door when a large, bony fist closed about her wrist.

'Just what do you think you are doing here, young woman?' barked out an unpleasant male voice.

Rosa jumped back, startled, and looked up to see the tall, gaunt figure of that dreadful Super Master, Mr Smart.

She felt inclined to tell him that it was none of his business. After all, she was almost a principal now and certainly not under his control, thank goodness. But she knew it was not wise to make enemies in the theatre. She held her temper and instead explained, 'I have to tell Mr Houghton what caused this.' She revealed the gaping tear in her trousers.

'Cover yourself up, woman,' Smart hissed, leaning over her and catching her full in the face with his whisky breath. 'You know you women are not supposed to wander about back-stage on your own. I'd have thought *you* had caused enough trouble doing that already!'

'I need to speak to Mr Houghton,' she said coldly, her anger rising again at the injustice of his remark.

'Someone else can do that. Tell the ASM or—'

'People forget,' she said, 'and anyway I have to explain the problems myself, properly.'

'Well, he's not there,' said Smart with some satisfaction, 'so you can't.'

You really are an appalling man, she thought.

'Well, where is he?'

'*I* don't know. In one of the upstairs property rooms, I expect, or down in the Property Cellar.'

'I'll look in both.'

'No you *won't*,' Smart retorted nastily.

'Oh yes I *will*,' she replied, anger having now taken over, 'and you can't stop me.'

She turned on her heel and began to walk away.

Like all bullies when defied he became confused. He caught up with her muttering, 'We'll get the blame if anything happens to you.'

She did not respond.

'Right, I'm coming with you, and that's that,' he announced finally. 'And Mr Barrett will hear all about this tomorrow.'

Rosa sighed and shrugged. 'Very well. If you must.'

Why hadn't she wakened the handsome young sergeant? At least he was pleasant company.

Smith, meanwhile, was back in the uniform of a Metropolitan Police Constable Third Class. He felt the constriction of the tight serge jacket around his chest and the scratch of its snug, high-buttoned collar around his neck.

Most of all he felt the anxiety of the new recruit, hoping he would not encounter a terrible accident around the next corner or a gang of costers who would take exception to his requests to cease their footway obstruction and beat him to death. And he had come out without his truncheon!

The rumbling sounds so loud to his ears were not, as in the scene in his head portrayed, the noise of the frantic goods and passenger traffic fighting to gain access to Paddington Railway Station. They were the trundling away of the *Lights o' London* scenery and the positioning of the first backdrop for the short popular farce, *A Photographic Fright*, which would start tomorrow evening's programme.

Rosa's expectations that Smith would soon be roused to follow her on her errands did not take into account the sympathies of the scene shifters. By common consent, they had decided to leave the poor lovesick fellow to slumber for as long as possible.

Smart and Rosa were deep among the typical after-show mayhem of the supers' dressing room. Sweaty figures bumping into each other as they fought for space to disrobe and remove wigs and stage make-up.

After checking with the stage-doorkeeper that Houghton had not yet left, Smart had insisted that Rosa acquire some sort of covering 'for decency's sake'. They might, he had pointed out, bump into the vestiges of the audience as they went to the property rooms on the upper floors.

She was now donning the long overall of the bloater and

whelk seller, thankful that although it looked suitably smeared and grubby it did not smell of the wares she had been offering, they being fakes produced by Mr Houghton in his workshop.

After Smart's insistence that he accompany her it had suddenly occurred to Rosa that the unpleasant Super Master might be just the person who murdered young women. Though irritated by the time-wasting, she had been reassured about his intentions when he dragged her into the supers' dressing room. Now everyone knew she was with him, so that must be all right.

They were about to leave at last when the Borough Market greengrocer grabbed Smart's arm complaining that one of the drunks was not only obscuring him and his wares but that the man's inebriated rantings were preventing his sales shouts from being heard.

The drunk in question, now busy removing blacking from his front teeth, turned around and exclaimed, 'Don't be so stupid. It's not as if you're really trying to sell any of them turnips and cabbages and goin' home empty handed to a starving wife and kids.'

He hooted with laughter at his own wit. He was joined in this by a flower seller and one of the prettier drabs who were peeping over the screen between them.

The greengrocer reddened angrily.

'No, but you could do me out of a job here, couldn't you, you bastard!'

'Shut up the pair of you!' yelled Smart.

'An' it's spoiling the scene,' the greengrocer went on, adding vehemently, 'an' Mr Barrett won't like it when I tell 'im.'

That stopped Smart in his tracks. He began to reason with the men. Rosa, already baulking at the delay, seized her opportunity while the Super Master was diverted by this territorial dispute and slipped away among a group of home-going supers. Once out of the dressing room she made her way to the stairs.

Smith was about to be run over by a slat-sided, Great Western Railway, horse-drawn wagon which, he was certain, was carrying over the recognized weight limit for one horse – one and three quarter tons.

He had stood in front of the vehicle, held up his hand and remonstrated with the driver. But the man had shouted abuse at him, raised his whip and brought it down hard on the poor horse's flank with the clear intention of driving the whole disputed weight over the body of Constable Smith.

He was saved at the very last moment by someone shaking his shoulder and shouting, 'Wake up! It's time to go! We need that chair.'

It was Harry Edgar at whom a dazed Smith smiled gratefully, relieved not to feel the weight of the iron-clad wheels crushing him as he tried to work out where on earth he was.

He glanced about him at the empty stage and the new backdrop and suddenly he realized.

'Rosa!' he exclaimed.

'Don't worry – ' Harry grinned – 'your lady friend said to tell you that she was going up to wardrobe and then she was off 'ome.'

Smith jumped to his feet and rushed towards the nearest stairs, then stopped abruptly and made his way to the stage door instead.

'Do not, under any circumstances,' he instructed the stage-doorkeeper by shouting over the heads of the departing throng, 'let Miss Drake go until I get back. Tell her she *must* wait for me!'

'Righto!' said the doorman, nodding but wondering how he was supposed to do that, women being such contrary creatures and he being of such a lowly rank.

Thirty-Six

R osa had intended to go up to the Property Room on the dress-circle floor then on to those on the upper-circle and amphitheatre levels. But at the last minute she changed her mind and decided it would be more sensible to go first to the Property Cellar, which was nearer.

She knew that the basement passages were a labyrinth leading to coal and wine cellars, the Band Room and the Gasman's Room as well as the Carpenter's Shop and the Property Cellar.

To avoid becoming lost, Rosa went down the stairs in the front hall, which led directly to the cul-de-sac where the Carpenter's Shop and the Property Cellar were situated.

The last of the bandsmen and under-stage workers made way for her as they emerged from their subterranean quarters, some giving her curious glances obviously wondering where she was going.

The Property Cellar was isolated at the very end of the passageway which lay directly under the scene dock. Rosa knocked hard on the door but there was no answer. She knocked again, harder this time, the sound echoing in the silent enclosed passage. Still no response. She tried the handle. To her relief the door opened. Houghton must be here. Despite her previous certainty that she was in no danger she had been starting to become a little nervous.

She knew that no one else would be down here until the gas engineer completed his final rounds switching off the gas with his key followed by the few oil lamps kept lit to prevent total darkness engulfing them should there be a gas explosion or failure.

Rosa was further relieved to hear the sound of two voices at the far end of the cellar. They were muffled somewhat by the stacked wooden crates, tin chests, piles of papier-mâché rocks, huge pantomime heads and the floral wreaths and torches designed to be carried aloft by the ballet dancers.

As she found her way around these obstructions she recognized one of the voices as that of the Property Master, Mr Houghton. He was a strange man who, although acknowledged to be good at his job, was, as the young actresses could testify, sometimes impertinent.

Indeed, she had been astonished when only the other day

he had informed her that no decent women would wear breeches and advised her not to play such roles any more! She did not recognize the other voice.

Their conversation sounded a little heated as if they were having a disagreement of some kind. No matter. At least there were two of them. There was nothing to fear from two men.

Once she had described her problem she would ask one of them to see her back upstairs. Then she would go home, leaving notes at the stage door for the wardrobe mistress and Sergeant Smith.

It was 11.15 p.m. and Best had just begun walking back down Ossulston Street after spending a sad evening with the bereft parents of Jerry Banks.

They could only tell him what he already knew too well, that their son had been besotted with Esther Gibbons and distraught when she went missing. They repeated endlessly that he would never have hurt her. He tended to believe them except that he knew how sudden anger and a broken heart could lead to even the mildest of men becoming violent.

He had stayed with the Gibbonses much longer than duty demanded because they wanted to talk about Jerry and were obviously dreading the agonizing empty silence that would descend on them once he left.

As he continued down towards Euston Road, his mind went back to the start of all this mess. Their night at the theatre, a rare treat for the busy pair, and the onstage murder of the pathetic foundling super, Talisman.

Which brought him back to the biggest puzzle of all and one they had still not solved: the gun.

Why had no one seen the exchange of the stage gun for the real weapon? Or seen the shot being fired? It was a puzzle. The only conclusion he could come to was that the person handling either of the guns was someone who normally did so at that point – and that was Barrett.

He had been taken in by the man's charm, confidence and seeming innocence as well as the unlikelihood of him bringing such trouble on his own production.

186

Why, also, had Barrett not taken charge sooner on the night of the tragedy? What was he doing?

I'm losing my touch, Best thought. I should not have been so easily hoodwinked. I should have stuck to the evidence and worked backwards from there and seen where it pointed. And here he was urging Smith to think things through!

Tomorrow, he decided, he would sit down and work out the case against Barrett.

Before starting for home Best decided to go into King's Cross Road Police Station and ask them to telegraph the Yard to see whether any messages had been left for him.

It was unlikely, of course, given the static state of the inquiry, but one never knew.

To his surprise there was a message from Smith. It had been left earlier in the evening and was marked Urgent. It's content startled him. 'Come to the theatre at once,' it said simply and abruptly. What on earth could that be about?

Well, the Princess's would be closing now unless they were holding some of their late-night rehearsals and he doubted that since no other production was imminent. Nonetheless, the emergency must still exist or Smith would have telegraphed again.

He hailed a cab, showed his warrant card to the driver and ordered, 'Princess's Theatre as quickly as you can, please.'

Smart had not only washed his hands of Rosa but had begun worrying that his treatment of her might have been a mistake. After all, she now had the ear of Barrett and she herself, it was said, was destined for the heights. She might take revenge on him. He argued with himself that it had been for her own good and she would realize that. But the doubt, once sewn, remained and took root.

He solved this dilemma as he did most others. He went for a drink.

Meanwhile, Smith, having received no response from any of the empty, silent, wardrobe rooms, was sick with worry.

He ran back down to the stage door where the rotund little red-faced doorkeeper insisted that he had not seen Rosa leave but was sure that Mr Barrett had gone home.

What should he do now? Best had told him that potassium cyanide could act in seconds. Rosa could be dead already!

There was only one thing he could do now.

'Close that door,' he ordered, pointing to the exit out on to Castle Street East. 'Don't let anyone else leave.'

'What?' exclaimed the doorkeeper incredulously. 'I can't do that!'

His eyes were wide and his face grew redder.

'Oh yes you can!' retorted Smith. 'Do as I say. Close that door and send someone to shut the others as well. No one is leaving until I find Miss Drake.'

The doorkeeper was still objecting loudly and doing nothing, so Smith held up his hand to stop the few stragglers from going through, then went to the door, undid the bolts which held it open, banged it closed and locked it, placing the key in his pocket.

He realized that there must be another key somewhere, so he turned to the doorkeeper again and threatened, 'If you open that before I tell you and let anyone through, I will see you charged with obstructing police in the execution of their duty!' He glanced around at the growing knot of grumbling supers and backstage workers who were wanting to know what was going on.

'Be quiet,' Smith barked at them. 'This is serious. Miss Drake is missing and may be in danger.'

A hush fell over the group at this.

'Have any of you seen her since the performance?'

There was a general shaking of heads but the super who played the prettier prostitute spoke up.

'Mr Smart brought her into our dressing room to get a coat to cover herself. She had torn her breeches.'

'Yes, I know about the breeches. Where did they go then?'

She shook her head. 'I don't know. But I saw her sneaking off while Mr Smart was sorting out a row between a couple of supers. Looked like she wanted to get away from him.' She glanced around her as she said it to make sure the all powerful Super Master was not nearby. 'Don't blame her,' she added when she found he wasn't and the other woman agreed, making faces at each other at the very idea of their leader.

'He was furious when he realized,' one of them put in.

'Right. Arrange yourselves into a group for each floor, then go and search for her. Look everywhere, everywhere, every corner, cupboard, trunk and,' he added, 'keep an eye open for Mr Smart as well.' He wanted to add that they should detain him if they found him but doubted they would dare.

The rapid clip-clop of the horse's hoofs and the rattle of its harness sent the tired Best off into a reverie. He could do nothing until he got to the theatre and found out what was going on, so he let the conundrum of who did what with the gun, the dangers to actresses wearing breeches and the threat of poison drift to the back of his mind as they sped along the Euston Road.

His idle gaze took in the numerous hotels (both private and temperance), the boarding houses, coffee rooms, cocoa rooms, oyster rooms and small manufacturers. A surprising number of the latter were producers of musical instruments or parts thereof, from pianoforte makers to accordion pleaters. The Euston Road also served the more basic needs of both the living and the dead with its many potato and coal merchants on the one hand and statuaries and monumental masons on the other.

It was one of the latter which lit Best's fuse in a roundabout manner. He was reflecting that it must be a strange way to spend your life, chipping away at stone and marble to produce memorials that then stood in a cemetery where few would notice them, never mind judge them for their artistic merit.

But didn't they say that working with your hands could be very satisfying?

A monumental mason would not have to worry about solving apparently unsolvable crimes. Then again, look at the Princess's Property Master. No one worked with their hands more than he but it didn't seem to make him happy. Resentful more like because he worked so hard.

Houghton!

He stood in the wings holding a dummy gun during the last act! His intention was to fire it off should the one on stage fail to make the required noise.

189

People were used to seeing him there. No one would find anything strange in the sight! Best recalled that when the rabble rushed in to besiege the police station they had done so from the wings – where Houghton stood.

He could have picked up the stage prop gun as the scene changed, then fired the real one into the back of Talisman's head just as the super went charging out on to the stage. The impetus would carry him forward just far enough to fall, exactly where his body had lain. The gun would have been thrown after him.

The light in the wings was dim and the stage hands would be too busy to notice what he was doing. No one had realized that anything was wrong until several moments later. After the deed, Houghton could simply withdraw – as he always did.

Why, thought Best, did I not think of him before? Because he was nowhere near the stage when the body was discovered?

He stretched up, tapped on the roof of the cab and shouted, 'Faster, cabbie, please. Faster!'

Thirty-Seven

As she approached, it became evident that the argument was growing more heated.

'You must be careful. Show a little sense!' admonished the other man. His voice was higher in tone than Houghton's and rather querulous. Rosa was surprised that the Property Master would let *anyone* speak to him like that unless, of course, they were management.

'I *am* careful,' insisted Houghton. 'Or I would have been caught by now, wouldn't I?' he added smugly.

They must be talking about the flouting of one of the

theatre's endless rules. Whichever one it was, it was better that they didn't know that she had overheard them.

To stop them saying any more she called out breezily, 'Mr Houghton, are you there?'

The other man, who had been speaking again, stopped abruptly. All was quiet for a few moments.

'Mr Houghton?'

'I'm here, my dear,' he called out. At that moment she rounded a stack of spears and halberds to see the Property Master standing there at the end of the cellar, quite alone.

'We've been waiting for you,' he said, and grinned.

The doors of the Princess's Theatre were all shut. This surprised Best, who seemed to recall that usually they should still be putting the scenery away and turning off all the lights. Surely, the last of the workmen and the actors who had stayed on for a drink in the dress-circle bar would not have gone home yet?

He tried the Oxford Street entrance first, then the pit door in Winsley Street and, finally, the stage door in Castle Street East. All were locked.

Best shrugged and was about to leave when he hesitated and glanced at his watch again. He was certain he was right. The theatre should not be locked and barred yet. Had something terrible happened?

He put his ear to the stage door and caught the faint sound of murmuring voices.

Suddenly a louder, more commanding male voice ordered, 'You must be systematic. Take note of where you've looked.'

John George!

Best banged hard on the door and shouted but could not make himself heard. He tried again, banging so hard that he skinned his knuckles. The voices hushed for a moment then Smith shouted, 'You can't come in! We're closed!'

'Not to me!' Best shouted back. 'It's Inspector Best! Let me in.'

Instantly, the bolts were drawn back and he heard the key being inserted in the lock.

Smart suddenly appeared alongside him, reeking of whisky.

'I've been trying to get back in as well,' he complained. 'What the hell does that policeman of yours think he's doing in there?'

What indeed? thought Best.

Smith had never been so glad to see Best in all his life but his attention was riveted on Smart.

'Where is she?' he demanded frantically.

'Who?'

'Miss Drake!'

'I dunno,' said Smart carelessly, his words falling over each other. 'The bitch ran away from me an' I was only trying to protect her.' With the back of his hand he wiped away the spittle that had gathered around his mouth. 'Thanks I get,' he muttered drunkenly. 'Typical.'

Smith did not have time for patience. He seized Smart by the shoulders and shook him. 'Where was she going? She's not in any of the wardrobe rooms and she hasn't left the theatre.'

Smart waved his hand dismissively. 'She weren't going to no wardrobe rooms.'

'Where, then?' Smith shook the man again. 'Where?'

'Property rooms,' Smart said. 'Looking for Houghton.'

'Oh, God,' said Best.

Smith looked at him. 'He's our man?'

Best nodded.

'Which rooms?' Smith asked quietly, holding in his fury with great difficulty. '*Which* property rooms?'

Smart was having difficulty gathering his thoughts and he made as though to sit down.

Smith struck him across the face. 'Which rooms? Which bloody rooms!'

Smart staggered back, then muttered sulkily, 'All of them 'cept the one here.'

'You – ' Smith pointed to the now large group of stragglers which had formed – 'search the upper rooms. We – ' he looked at Best – 'will take the cellar.'

Best nodded, then held up his hand to stop them and said, 'If you see Houghton, detain him.'

Smith began to run towards the auditorium and the same stairs earlier taken by Rosa. He was almost in tears as he turned his head towards Best and said, 'We'll be too late. I know we'll be too late.'

Best said nothing. Just tried to keep up with the younger man.

As they burst into the Property Cellar, they heard raised voices at the far end, as had Rosa. Like her, as they drew nearer they recognized one of them as that of Houghton.

'He's here,' exclaimed Smith as he pushed his way through the long, low room. 'Please God, she is too and is all right.'

When they reached Houghton they found him alone, as had Rosa. This was the end of the cellar and there was no one else in sight. Houghton's head was bent to his task – cutting up a dark blue overall with a large pair of scissors.

He turned, startled. 'What do you want?'

'Where is she?' shouted Smith.

'Who?'

'Miss Drake!'

'That slut,' said Houghton and went back to his task. Then he grinned suddenly and said, 'We're not going to tell them, are we?'

'Why should we?' said the other voice. It, too, was coming from Houghton's mouth. His face now wore a different expression; harder, disdainful.

'You shut up,' replied Houghton, 'always butting in when you're not wanted.'

'You couldn't do without me,' sneered the second voice. 'You always want to have all the fun yourself. Well, I'm not going to let you . . .'

The voices went on and on, quarrelling. Best and Smith looked at each other in horror.

'Oh, God,' said Best. 'The man's raving. We'll never get anything out of him.'

Smith tried, by means of brute force, but it was hopeless.

At that moment a slightly soberer Smart came up behind them.

193

'That was the coat she was wearing,' he said, pointing to the results of Houghton's cutting exercise.

'Then she must be down here,' said Smith. 'He hasn't had enough time to take her anywhere else!'

Best sniffed. He could discern a sweetish odour in the stale air. 'What's that smell?'

Smart sniffed too. 'I recognize it,' he said. 'But I can't think . . .' He stopped. 'I know, it's that stuff they sometimes use at the dentist's.'

'Nitrous oxide,' said Best, who had solved a rape case in which it had been used. 'He's anaesthetized her!' He stared around him.

'Open all the large crates and trunks, quickly,' he yelled. 'She could suffocate.'

Houghton giggled. 'They think we don't know what we're doing, don't they?'

The second voiced laughed too. 'But we worked it out, didn't we? We wanted to have more fun.'

Best felt the urge to beat Rosa's whereabouts out of the man but he knew it would be no use, so he began tearing through the trunks and crates.

Soon they stood helplessly regarding the debris of torn-off crate lids and scattered contents.

What to do now? Best couldn't think. They had opened every container long enough to take a body.

'Perhaps he folded her up,' he said finally. In which case she is probably dead, he thought.

Out of nowhere came the memory of the scene in which Houghton was complaining about his multitudinous tasks.

'Find the bodies!' he yelled.

'What?' said Smith.

'Back there – we passed a pile of bodies!'

Best began to run back along the cellar, Houghton's shouts following him. He tried to hold Smith back, yelling, 'She's mine! She's mine!'

Smith turned, felled him with an uppercut, and ran after Best.

He was astonished to see Best climbing up a pile of 'corpses'; some were hard, papier-mâché shells, others were

194

made of cotton which was stuffed like a doll's body.

'A train wreck, an explosion, them bodies that are going to be flung about – I make them,' Houghton had said.

Best, concerned that the pile might topple, stopped Smith from climbing up with him. He looked about him. Where to start? Then he heard it. He held up his hand.

'Shush. Keep quiet.'

A faint coughing came from one of the papier-mâché female corpses just behind him. Its hard shell had been cut in two lengthwise and holes pierced in the lid. Best prised it open to reveal a drowsy dishevelled Rosa trying to sit up.

He untied her hands and feet and slowly pulled her out while Smith got a purchase on the pile halfway up. Between them they guided her to the ground and lowered her on to a throne intended for one of Shakespeare's monarchs.

Smith was almost in tears again, this time of relief when he saw she was alive.

'She must go to the hospital immediately,' Best said, turning to Smart. 'Get a cab and send some men down to help carry her up. Anaesthetics can be dangerous, especially in the wrong hands.'

A cackle of laughter came from behind them. Houghton was coming round and shouting, 'We know what we were doing. She won't die!'

'She'd better not,' Smith shouted back.

Thirty-Eight

'So, John George was right after all,' said Helen as she handed Best a steaming plate of onion soup.

Best nodded. 'Absolutely.'

'I trust you praised him?'

'To the skies. Heaped it on the young man's head. He was

quite startled, I can tell you, particularly when Cheadle joined in.'

'It was well deserved.'

'Yes. But there wouldn't have been such a crisis if he hadn't gone to sleep at the wrong time again. He has a guardian angel, that lad.'

They both recalled the time Smith had fallen asleep in St Pancras Railway Station while searching for a murderess, woken up in a panic and then caught her just as she was about to board a train.

'If he *hadn't* gone to sleep you wouldn't have caught Houghton.'

'Yes, we would. I had just realized that it must be him.' Best grinned. 'You know, I only just stopped the lad confessing to his nap. Fortunately, Rosa felt so guilty about causing such a commotion that she told everyone she had given him the slip.'

Helen shook her head. 'When first we practise to deceive . . .'

'We join the CID,' said Best. 'I've told you, a little inno- cent deceit is part of the job. It helps us catch bad people.'

'Ha!' said Helen.

'If I'd let him confess John George would not have got his promotion to First Class Sergeant, and you wouldn't want that, would you?'

'No,' she admitted. 'I'm glad. They need the money.'

It was their first opportunity to exchange news for several days, Best being caught up in the aftermath of the arrest, which, as usual, almost seemed to take as long as the case itself.

Rosa was now out of hospital and, despite exhortations to rest, was back at the Princess's, still playing her breeches role. Houghton was safely ensconced in one of Her Majesty's asylums for the insane.

'Still no sign of Ida?' Helen asked.

Best paused and said, 'Lovely soup this. Must tell Jessie—'

Helen stopped ladling her own portion and glared at him. 'Ernest!'

He sighed and put down his soup spoon. 'I don't want to upset you.'

'You'll upset me more if you don't tell me.'

'All right, all right. But I've warned you.'

'Go on.'

'There was a full set of female bones inside one of the papier-mâché corpses.'

Helen sat down, still holding the ladle. 'Oh, how sad.'

'Obviously, he had been able to get rid of the flesh long since in his workshop, so there is no way of telling whose bones they are but the medical men say they belonged to a young woman.'

'Do you think there will be any more?'

'I hope not. We don't know of any other actresses missing like that but who knows?'

'I wonder why only those two should be selected out of all the women who have played breeches roles?'

'Three, really, counting Rosa.' He shook his head. 'It's a mystery. It seems we'll never know unless Houghton recovers his senses and confesses.'

Helen considered this while eating her soup but Best knew by her preoccupied expression that more questions were coming.

'There are four things which still puzzle me,' she said eventually. 'Why Houghton murdered Talisman, why the other supers gave him those bruises, who sent the blackmail letters to Barrett and what they were about and why Houghton decided to put Esther's body out in the open instead of disposing of it quietly in his workshop as he could have done?'

'Well, in fact he did tell us in a roundabout way why he killed Talisman. When he and his other self were arguing they began complaining about that interfering super. It was obvious from what they said that Talisman must have discovered him trying to trap Esther and was going to tell Barrett.

'The reason he put Esther's body out in the open like that was probably, as that wise young man Smith deduced, he wanted to show off his work and to frighten the actresses into not playing these roles.'

'But that was the only one they saw. So how would they know why they were murdered?'

'They would start to realize when the next body appeared

'– Rosa's – and he would probably have left a few more clues with it, like the pipe and the cap.'

'Oh, dear,' said Helen. 'How dreadful.'

He hurried on before she had time to contemplate that dreadful scenario. 'As for that business of the supers turning on Talisman and the blackmail of Barrett, they go together.'

He held out his plate for a refill and explained, 'We eventually got it out of the supers – by fear of mass dismissal – that Houghton had told them that Talisman was in line for all the good utility roles coming up by virtue, if you'll excuse the word, of his relationship with Barrett.'

'By relationship, you mean?'

He nodded. 'Yes.'

'And the blackmail letters also suggested the relationship and threatened to expose it?'

He nodded again. 'That's right.'

'Any truth in it?'

He laughed. 'I shouldn't think so!'

'But what was the point of turning the supers against Talisman and blackmailing Barrett?'

'To confuse us, to muddy the water.' Best laughed. 'He wasn't to know we would be so dilatory following up both these matters – not to mention overlooking his own obvious role as a man holding a gun.'

'I think you're being a little hard on yourselves. It was such a complicated scene you were thrown into and a world you knew nothing about.'

'Hmm,' muttered Best, who believed in facing up to your mistakes and trying to learn from them, no matter how painful it proved.

'One thing is certain,' he said finally.

'What's that, my love?'

'The next time I'm in a theatre and an actor dies on stage I'm going to tell them I'm off duty and sneak away home.'

Author's Note

Wilson Barrett, E. S. Willard, Miss Eastlake, Mrs Stephens, Miss Emmeline Ormsby, G. R. Sims and the Bancrofts were all real people and their shades must forgive me for throwing a suspicion of guilt on some of them. Littlechild, Williamson and Vincent are also the genuine article.

The Lights o' London ran for two hundred and twenty-six performances. Barrett had a further great success with *The Silver King,* which followed the less popular *The Romany Rye.* He left the Princess's in 1886 to tour in North America and later Australia. In 1895, when melodrama had begun to lose some of its popularity, he scored another resounding success with his own religious play, *The Sign of the Cross.* He died in 1904.

George R. Sims continued working as a crusading journalist, notably on his collection of articles published in book form as *How the Poor Live* (1889). He was also the author of several crime stories, some of which featured Dorcas Dene, Detective. Dorcas was a former actress.

Sims was once mistaken for Jack the Ripper and claimed to know the man's identity, possibly through his contact with Littlechild. And he really did walk from St Albans to London or at least claimed he did!

The fortunes of the Princess's Theatre gradually waned and it was closed down in 1902. Part of the premises were given over to shops and the auditorium became a furniture store. Later, a branch of Woolworth's was erected there, followed by a shopping complex. Today, there is an HMV music and DVD store on the site. At the rear is Princess House, in which my agent, Juliet Burton, once worked.

Acknowledgements

M y thanks to the London Metropolitan Archives, where I was able to peruse the architectural plans for the Princess's Theatre (1880s building) and hold some of the slips of paper that the Foundling Hospital had given mothers in exchange for their babies.

At the Theatre Museum I found much information regarding the real life characters in this book plus *The Lights o' London* scene illustrations, playbills and programmes. The British Library supplied the original playscript (which had been casually jotted down on scraps of lined paper) and the first printed version in *The Lights o' London & Other Victorian Plays*, Editor: Michael R. Booth (OUP World Classics, 1995). Interestingly, in the original version it is the villain who is called Harold while the hero's name is George.

What initially fired my interest in the subject was a marvellous collection of nineteenth-century articles on all aspects of the *Victorian Theatre*, in a book of that name by Russell Jackson (A&C Black, 1989).

Other particularly useful works were *The Rise of the Victorian Actor* by Michael Baker (Croom Helm, 1978), *The Lost Theatres of London* by Raymond Mander and Joe Mitchenson (New English Library, 1976) and *Ellen Terry: Player in Her Time* by Nina Auerbach (Phoenix House, 1987). This last is most vocal on the question of breeches roles.

Grateful thanks also to fellow crime novelist Michael Jecks for information on Victorian firearms.

J. L.